A
HARLEQUIN
Book

FEAST OF
THE CANDLES

by

IRIS DANBURY

HARLEQUIN BOOKS

Winnipeg • Canada   New York • New York

FEAST OF THE CANDLES

First published in 1968 by Mills & Boon Limited,
50 Grafton Way, Fitzroy Square, London, England.

Harlequin Canadian edition published May, 1970
Harlequin U.S. edition published August, 1970

Standard Book Number: 373-51398-4.

Printed in Canada

CHAPTER ONE

ANTONIA had been in Perugia long enough to know that in this Italian hilltop town there was always a wind blowing. No doubt in the hot August days one would welcome a cool breeze, but on this early-April evening she pulled her warm white coat around her as she hurried along the Corso Vannucci, the main street. Yet in spite of the chilliness, she could never resist pausing for a moment to sniff the delicious aroma that drifted out of the corner shop where the famous Perugina chocolates were sold.

A girl with short dark hair, smoke-grey eyes and a pale skin that had clearly not yet experienced Italian summer sunshine, she was not noticeably English, for at this time of year Perugia's universities were full of foreign students from all over Europe.

She continued down the Corso until it ended at the great square, the Piazza Republica. She leaned over the stone balustrade on top of the old Etruscan walls and gazed at the superb panorama spread out below, the lesser hills in the distance each crowned with its historic town, the wide, undulating plain, the sky tinted with lilac, amethyst and tawny orange.

Here was the sense of illimitable space and tranquillity strangely at odds with the turbulent history of this medieval town perched on its several hills dominating the valley.

Although, in common with most of the inhabitants of Perugia, Antonia came almost every evening to this "grand balcony" as she called it, she rarely failed to remember with gratitude and appreciation that she owed the opportunity to her godfather, Philip Canford, who had provided her with both money and leisure.

"You're twenty-one," he had told her that afternoon in her mother's sitting-room. "I'm prepared to give you now the legacy you'd inherit on my death.

But," he added a warning, "there are conditions."

"You haven't picked out someone you want me to marry, have you?" she asked, smiling at him.

"No, hardly that. It's just that I shall expect you to spend a year in Italy, wandering around the towns, Rome, Florence, Milan, Naples and the rest—and paint."

She had been overwhelmed by his generosity and said so.

"Oh, I've my own axe to grind," he replied. "If you have anything of the real artist in you then I want to see something of it before I die, and I'm not yet an old man. Even if you never make the grade, you'll have had the opportunity of a fling."

"A marvellous opportunity," she had whispered, almost speechless with surprise. "I promise I won't waste it."

"When you come back you'll know for certain whether you can spend most of your time being a professional artist or try something else."

Antonia had recently finished her art training and gained a diploma that would qualify her for teaching. When Philip's offer came, she had been on the point of accepting a post in a girls' school on the East Coast, but with the least delay she booked a flight to Rome.

Her mother had expressed a certain amount of anxiety at the idea of Antonia's going off alone for a whole year, but Philip, a very old friend of the family, had smoothed that out.

In Rome she spent a month sightseeing and studying in the museums, then visited Florence, which enchanted her. Resolutely she stayed only three weeks' fearing that she might never see the rest of Italy. She knew that she would return.

Sheer chance had brought her to Perugia, for on a visit to Assisi she had been intrigued by the distant town on its hilltop. Perugia had claimed her for more than a month. But that was partly due to Robert Ellard, the young assistant manager of the Hotel Margharita where she had first stayed. He was living for a

6

year in Perugia to continue his training in the hotel industry and to perfect his Italian.

It was his suggestion that she should learn the language.

"There are short courses at the University for people like you," he told her one evening. "There's no better place to learn almost any language. People come here from all over Europe."

"Oh, I don't know—" she began dubiously.

"Don't be lazy," he scolded. "Artists like you need something to discipline them. Otherwise you'll spend your time painting only when you feel like it or else mooning about the museums."

So she had taken his advice and enrolled at the University for foreigners in the old Gallenga Palace for the beginners' course. As Robert had pointed out, even a simple basic everyday knowledge of Italian would help her to talk to far more people in the rest of Italy when she moved away from Perugia.

She turned away from the Piazza and walked towards the Hotel Margharita close by. She had soon found that the hotel would prove too expensive for her for any length of stay and Robert had recommended a small *albergo* in a side street where she had a pleasant room with a balcony and could buy her breakfast and other meals at cafés as she chose.

In the covered courtyard of the Margharita she glanced around at the tables where people sat drinking coffee or aperitifs. Robert rose from a corner table and came towards her.

"Hallo, Antonia," he greeted her. "Glad you could come."

He ordered drinks for them both and she waited for the news he had promised her.

"How many pictures have you painted since you came to Italy?" he queried.

"Only five or six," she answered. "Of those only two are finished, but they're not yet ready for varnishing."

7

His expression became thoughtful. "I see," he murmured.

"Why? Have you found me a rich buyer or a discriminating dealer?"

Robert grunted. "Not exactly, but I thought I could arrange for some of your pictures to be exhibited for a time in a small studio here, so that your work could be seen."

"I don't think I'm really up to exhibition standard yet," she said.

After a pause he said, "Oh, well, perhaps we can do something later on."

She accompanied him into the restaurant for dinner and noticed with what deference he was served, even though tonight he was off duty.

He asked about her progress in Italian.

She began to giggle. "I make the most absurd mistakes," she said. "The Professor is such a good actor that sometimes he confuses me. We were learning about clocks and telling the time. He waved his arm at the wall and I told him he was wearing a wall clock instead of a wrist-watch."

Robert laughed, too.

"But I wasn't the only one to make mistakes. The Greeks never do, they've been chattering away in Italian since the end of the first week, but the Swedish girl makes wild guesses. The three German men write down everything three times over and check it with each other before they say anything on their own."

"Aren't there any other Anglo-Saxons in your class?" Robert queried. "I thought you said there were some Americans."

"Oh, yes, but the woman from Boston just sits and beams happily, the two American men are regretting that they didn't start Italian when they were ten years old. The Indian girl has chummed up with the two Danes, and the Spaniard is quite taken with a very pretty Swiss girl."

Robert smiled. "You can't complain that the classmates are dull. At least they have international variety.

Soon I shall expect you to converse with me entirely in Italian."

"*Non domani,*" she said. "Certainly not tomorrow nor the next day."

During the meal she wondered if she had been right in sacrificing even a few weeks of her "Italian Year" to language lessons when she ought to have been painting. Already it seemed that she had lost one opportunity of having her work shown.

"Robert," she said suddenly, "I was thinking about this little exhibition. I have some line drawings that I've made in Perugia. Would they be of any use?"

He sipped his cognac. "I don't see why you couldn't display them," he answered slowly. "You won't sell them, of course, but I've had another idea, too. I might be able to persuade a man I know to look at your paintings with a critical eye. Then you could accept or reject his advice before you finish them, since they're not varnished."

"Would he waste his time, do you think? I'm still only a novice."

"So was he once and he's very helpful to young artists."

She and Robert returned to the lounge bar for coffee and liqueurs when suddenly Robert jumped up hastily with a murmured excuse and walked across to greet a tall man who had just entered. For a couple of moments the two men chatted together, then Robert brought his companion to Antonia.

"Antonia," he said, "you might like to meet Talbot Drury. He's an archaeologist and likes nothing so much as rummaging about in the soil for what he can find." He glanced towards the tall, broad-shouldered man with the fair hair and blue eyes. "Miss Antonia Meade is an artist making the Grand Tour of Italian cities."

"Not in the least," she objected, shaking her head. "Only a would-be artist trying to see something of Italy."

The two men sat down and Robert ordered more coffee and cognac.

"When do you expect to start digging?" he asked Talbot.

"As soon as I can get a team together, but my assistant Stefano is handling that side for me. I was fortunate, apparently, to find him. He was recommended to me by a friend, and since he lives not far from here he ought to know the district well."

Antonia, pouring coffee, took no part in the conversation until Robert explained, "Talbot has worked in Persia, Turkey and Greece. Now he's come here to find out about Etruscan traces."

"Etruscan?" echoed Antonia. "Those who were here before the Romans. The very word sounds mysterious. I must read up their history."

Talbot gave her an interested glance. "Very little is known about it. So much has been built on top of the old Etruscan cities—Roman, medieval and the rest—that it's difficult to find much authentic evidence of what they were like."

"But you hope to make some discoveries," put in Robert.

"Of course. I'd like to turn up more than just a few urns. There are dozens of those in various museums."

"Where are you going to start?" asked Robert.

"Possibly on the north side of Perugia. I think the southern slopes between here and Assisi have been well worked over, and it struck me last autumn when I stayed here for a few days on my way home from Greece that there might be more finds to the east and north."

A few minutes later he rose, saying that he had to visit Stefano and discuss details with him. When he had gone, Antonia commented, "I never imagined a *young* archaeologist—well, comparatively young. Usually they seem to be greybeards."

Robert laughed. "Talbot Drury will probably be a greybeard in due course, but he's apparently made a name for himself in excavation circles."

"Is he staying here all the time he's on this expedition?" she asked.

"I think so. He's booked a suite for a couple of months anyway. He also takes one of our small storerooms for stowing what he finds. He needs a place where he can have the urns and pots and other pieces cleaned and fixed together."

When she left the Hotel Margharita with Robert, Antonia's head was full of imaginative fancies about ancient civilisations and the modern young men who delighted in the hard work of revealing and preserving the traces that still remained.

"Goodnight, Antonia." Robert's voice recalled her to the fact that he had already escorted her to the door of the small inn where she lived.

"*Buona notte*," she ventured. "*Arrivederci*."

"Don't forget about those drawings," he reminded her. "Bring them to me at the Margharita tomorrow if you can. I'll have to let you know about the paintings and make an appointment when Vittorio can see them."

"Yes, I understand that. I'm very grateful to you, Robert."

When he had gone she hesitated in the vestibule before going up to her room. On a sudden impulse she went out into the street again, turned the opposite way from Robert's direction back to the Margharita and threaded her way through a maze of narrow streets until she came to one that descended sharply. Flights of worn stone steps led down at unexpected angles, and houses rose on either side of the steep alley so that ground floors were on the same level as chimney-pots of a neighbour two doors lower down.

She reached the last flight of steps, walked through the arch of the Etruscan Gate, then turned back to gaze at its floodlit magnificence. She had passed it many times on her way to and from the University, but now she began to sense its significance. Through this archway, one of the main entrances into the old walled city, travellers and citizens had passed more than two thousand years ago.

11

There could scarcely have been a greater contrast between the modern busy road where motor traffic coursed along and the immense arches and square towers of this silent monument bathed in amber radiance.

She became aware that someone had moved out of the shadows and was walking towards her.

"I think this is the second time we have met this evening," the man said, and as he turned his head his fair hair caught the light.

"Yes, Mr. Drury," she answered.

"Do you often come here to admire the Gate at this time of night?" he asked.

"Well, no," she admitted. "Robert—Mr. Ellard— accompanied me back to the place where I live, but I suddenly wanted to come out again and look at something that's ancient and hasn't had to be dug up."

"Sometimes it's only the fact that interesting buildings or parts of them have been buried under layers of dust that has preserved them for us to find. History is one long tale of destruction."

"But rebuilding, too, surely," she reminded him.

"Yes. Every king of the castle has built his triumphant fortress on the ruins of someone else's."

She smiled. "You're probably biased. Perhaps one day in the future archaeologists will wonder why we built skyscrapers like matchboxes on end."

She put out her hand to touch the surprisingly warm stonework and wondered about those other hands that built the towers and walls so long ago.

"It's fairly late," he said. "Perhaps you'll allow me to walk with you to your hotel."

"It's only a small inn," she told him, "but comfortable and cheap. That's the main thing."

"Then you're not staying at the Margharita?"

"I can't afford it for any length of time," she told him, and added a brief account of how she came to be in Perugia for perhaps a couple of months.

"My godfather has been generous," she continued, "and I want to make his gift last out the whole year.

12

Fortunately, he lets me have the money quarterly so that I have some idea of how to space it out."

"He sounds a far-seeing man as well as a generous one," Talbot Drury commented. "Are you painting here?"

"At the moment I'm taking a short elementary course in Italian at the University. After that I must use most of my time for painting."

They paused to recover breath, for ascending the steps was more tiring than lightly tripping down them. "Are you a good painter?" he queried.

"Not yet. And if I were, you wouldn't expect me to say so, would you?"

In the darkness she could not see his face, but she heard him laugh quietly. "No, I think you'd be modest enough for that."

"Are you a good archaeologist? I'm entitled to ask that in return, I hope?"

"Certainly. That is, you may ask. I'll admit only to being a reasonably good archaeologist. At first I studied mineralogy, but then I became more interested in uncovering fragments of old civilisations."

Soon they had reached the top of the narrow street, then walked along behind the cathedral and from there it was no distance to Antonia's *albergo*. At the entrance she said goodnight to Mr. Drury.

"Now that I've been brought home twice in one evening," she said, "I promise not to saunter out again."

In her room she reflected that so far she had been fortunate to meet two such attractive Englishmen in Perugia. Not that she was likely to see much of Mr. Drury once he started his excavations outside the city. Robert, on the other hand, with his warm, ready smile and kind brown eyes, could probably be counted on to help her out of most difficulties she might meet.

Early next morning she sorted out her drawings and paintings and assessed them with a critical eye. The line drawings she could probably tidy up this afternoon before she took them to Robert, but the paintings were mostly in a raw state and needed a good deal of work on them.

When she met Robert at the Margharita in the evening she said, "D'you think it might be possible for me to rent a share of a studio somewhere handy? I can't really use my bedroom and the balcony faces south, so the light's wrong."

Robert thought for a few moments while he studied the drawings. "Yes, I might be able to fix something," he said at last. "First, though, I want to get this exhibition properly arranged. Otherwise the whole project will fall to pieces as I have to go down to Rome in a couple of days."

"Oh. For long?" she queried.

"Only a few days, I think. I have to meet my cousin Cleo and her mother. They've been on a long holiday in Naples, Rome and other places. Now they're coming here for a week or two before going on to Florence."

Robert was on duty at the hotel this evening and could spare little time for entertaining Antonia, but this, of course, she understood, and after thanking him for his help, she left the Margharita and went to a café in the Piazza Dante.

She wondered what his cousin was like. With a name like Cleo she was probably tall and sophisticated, with sleek dark hair and elegant hands. The mother? Perhaps she was frail and unable to winter in England, although Antonia now realised that there were warmer places than most of Italy during the winter months.

Her thoughts as she idly drank her coffee were interrupted by two students from her Italian class, the Swedish girl, Ingrid, now accompanied by one of the Danes, usually called Sven. With such an international composition, most of Antonia's class-mates knew each other by Christian names and no longer bothered with surnames.

"Oh, how relaxing to talk English with someone!" exclaimed Ingrid. "My head is spinning with all those verbs and tenses. May we join you?"

"Of course," agreed Antonia as Sven borrowed a chair from another table. "It sounds odd to me to speak of relaxing in what is a foreign language for you," she added. She admired their fluent, perfect English.

"Oh, we learn it at school when we are too young to be frightened by funny sounds or spellings," Ingrid explained.

The two Scandinavians were both tall and blond. Sven was learning Italian because he liked travelling in Mediterranean countries and Ingrid had ideas about becoming an air hostess.

Sven ordered wine and the three chatted together, with occasional hilarious lapses into their imperfect Italian. Ingrid mimicked their Professor. Then she became suddenly serious.

"No, I am unkind to that nice man," she said. "He is a very good teacher of languages and I should be grateful to him."

It was late when the three companions parted and when she reached the Albergo Violetta where she lived. Antonia reflected that she would not have made so many friends here if she had not taken Robert's advice and joined the language class.

Toward the end of the week Robert telephoned that he had arranged for the exhibition. She wrote down the address he gave her.

"Is it a shop or an upstairs room?" she asked.

"A shop that displays paintings and pottery and so on, but there's a room at the back," he replied. "Your drawings will be shown for at least a week, possibly a fortnight, but go in and see the other exhibits whenever you can. You never know who you might meet there."

"Thank you very much, Robert. It's good of you to take so much trouble for me. I'll certainly go in and learn all I can."

"I'm off to Rome tomorrow morning," he told her, "but I hope to be back in three or four days." He laughed softly. "Timetables don't mean a lot to Cleo or her mother if they have other plans."

15

"Goodbye, Robert. Have a good trip."

The next day, Saturday, brought a merciful respite from Italian classes until Monday morning, and Antonia was eager to see her own work displayed for the first time, other than in end-of-term showing. She went to the address that Robert had given her, but was disappointed to find that the previous exhibits were only just being taken down. The penalty of vanity, she thought wryly, as she went out again into the street.

Unable to feast her eyes on her own triumphs, she decided to spend most of the week-end working on her paintings. She set up her easel just inside the french windows of her room so that she was able to stand on her balcony and move a step or two away. She saw glaring faults in the first picture and put it away hastily.

"What daubs!" she exclaimed to herself. "Have I learned nothing whatever in all those years at art school? Inwardly she hoped that even the few weeks she had spent in Italy had already given her higher standards of appreciation, a more fastidious appraisal of the good and the bad.

When she went the second time to the studio shop to see the exhibition, she discovered that paintings by several artists had been hung in the narrow back room behind the shop, but her drawings were nowhere to be seen.

She asked in her halting Italian what had happened to them.

"There was no room," the elderly man in charge told her. "The light, you understand?"

Naturally she understood that the best light must be reserved for colour work. Eventually she found the drawings fastened on a screen in an alcove, where it was unlikely that anyone would see them.

Antonia sighed. One must not expect wonders for a first showing and she was sure that Robert had done his best. She wandered from one picture to another, but disappointment prevented her from concentrating on style and technique, especially as the majority were abstracts.

She was studying a copy of a Perugino, part of his *Adoration of the Magi*, when a voice close beside her said, "*Buon giorno*, Miss Meade."

Mr. Drury was also studying the painting.

She turned quickly. "I didn't expect to see you in here," she said.

"I guessed that you might be. Robert said you had some drawings. Where are they?"

"Tucked away in a kind of cupboard," she whispered. "I'll show you."

"We'll alter that," he promised when she showed him the alcove.

In a few minutes he had summoned the proprietor and insisted in fluent but faulty Italian that the screen should be placed in a better light and more accessible.

"He'll probably hide them away again when we've gone," said Antonia.

"Maybe," Talbot Drury returned. "In the meantime, I want to see them without having to use a torch."

She waited while he examined the sketches. "I take it that you've done these sketches since you've been here," he said at last. "First hand? I mean, not copied from art books or other artists' work."

"Oh, yes," she replied at once, slightly indignant that he should think she had come all the way to Italy to copy what could be done in any good library.

"M'm," he muttered. "I wonder—would you care to come and have some coffee with me—that is, if you've finished your tour here."

"Thank you, yes. For the moment I've seen all I can."

He suggested the Margharita or somewhere along the Corso Vannucci and she chose the latter, a small place round a corner, where awnings protected the customers from cold winds and the shuffling, murmurous din of pedestrians in the main street.

"I'll come straight to the point," said Talbot, when the waiter had withdrawn. "I may need the services of an artist on my present project. Naturally, I have a photographer. Stefano, who will also be my chief assistant, is first-class in that direction. But I've found from experience that photographs can't always reveal the detail that establishes whether a particular find is worth while."

"I know absolutely nothing of archaeology," she said candidly.

"That's not important." His tone was brusque. "If I wanted you to sketch, say, a gas-cooker or a chair, I suppose you could do that reasonably accurately?"

"I think so," she agreed.

"There would be other people to decide on the archaeological merits. You'd work under Stefano, who would choose whether photographs or sketches would serve us better."

Antonia was silent for a while, thinking over this astounding offer. "How long are you intending to work in this part of Italy?" she asked at last.

"Most of the summer," he replied.

"I'm wondering if I could stay here so long," she murmured.

"Have you made plans to move on elsewhere?"

"Not yet. I probably shouldn't have stayed so long in Perugia if Robert hadn't persuaded me to take the language course."

"How long does that last?" he queried.

"About another five weeks. I'm taking only the short preparatory course for foreigners."

There was a long pause. Then Talbot said, "I gather you don't feel very enthusiastic about working on an archaeological project?"

"I might if I knew more about what was involved," she replied. "In any case, I should have to write to my godfather and let him know that I intended to stay here for some time."

"Of course," he agreed. "Will you do that?"

"I'll think about it." She smiled at him. "I've been given a year's supply of money so that I can paint. Philip, my godfather, may disapprove if I'm going to pursue every will o' the wisp that offers—first learning Italian all day, then dabbling in archaeology."

Talbot laughed and his broad shoulders shook. "It's the first time I've heard my life work described as a will o' the wisp!"

"Oh, I didn't mean to—" she began hastily.

"No, I'm sure you didn't. Everyone must have their own individual values. Perhaps you think that "digging" is like small boys playing with sand-castles."

"I'm not going to be drawn into answering that until I've seen what goes on at a site."

"Good. In a way I prefer people not to commit themselves too hastily, even to a will o' the wisp." He gave her a smile that was both friendly and faintly derisive.

They walked along the Corso to the 'balcony' at the far end. Talbot was more knowledgeable than she and could name the towns crowning their hills. "Deruta, Bettona," he pointed out. "Down there Assisi. It looks as though it's in a valley, but of course it's still quite high."

"Every town on a hilltop," she said, "to fend off its enemies."

When she left Talbot Drury and returned to her hotel, she found a message from Robert telling her that he was back and suggesting that she might like to come to the Margharita for dinner.

She was interested enough in Robert to want to meet his cousin and aunt; she was also appreciative of his friendliness in asking her to meet members of his family as soon as they arrived.

She dressed carefully in a daffodil-yellow two-piece that contrasted with her dark hair, chose a new make-up that gave her face a warm glow and, well pleased with her appearance, walked the short distance to the Hotel Margharita.

When she was introduced to Robert's aunt, Mrs. Norwood, and her daughter, Cleo, Antonia could scarcely prevent herself from uttering loud exclamations of surprise. She managed to school her face into an appropriate expression and hoped that no one had noticed her involuntary open-mouthed astonishment.

Far from being the elegant sophisticated creature of

19

Antonia's imagination, Cleo was small and blonde with long hair. Her pink-and-white fairness and greenish-tinged eyes gave her an almost kittenish appearance.

Talbot joined the small party after dinner and brought his assistant, Stefano, a dark-eyed Italian with a ready smile, who was delighted to find two young and pretty girls to add to his acquaintances. While Robert chatted to his aunt, Mrs. Norwood, with Talbot occasionally taking part, Stefano, seated happily between the two girls, divided his sparkling attention in a manner that flattered Cleo and amused Antonia.

"I simply haven't a notion how I'm ever going to learn much Italian," Cleo said, laughing at an obvious compliment that Stefano had made. "I struggle through '*Buon giorno*' and 'How much does it cost?' but I never understand the answers."

"Perhaps I may be permitted to become your teacher?" Stefano offered, following up his advantage.

Cleo smiled and dimpled provocatively, then caught Robert's eye. To Antonia's surprise, Robert was frowning and his face was a thunder-cloud.

It was Talbot who broke up the circle. "Stefano and I will leave now, if you'll excuse us. We have an early start tomorrow morning and a great deal of preparation."

Reluctantly, the young Italian rose and made his round of farewells. Antonia was uncertain whether she ought to go, too, but she did not want to make it apparent to Stefano that she was not resident at the Margharita, for she knew that he would instantly offer to escort her to the *albergo* and she was not inclined to give him too much encouragement.

After a suitable interval she said, "I must go home. It's late."

"You're not staying here, Miss Meade?" Mrs. Norwood asked. She was totally different from her daughter. In fact, she might have been the older edition of the elegant, soignée woman that Antonia had imagined Cleo would be.

She smiled now at Cleo's mother. "No. I came here

first, but it's rather too expensive for me for a long stay."

If the Norwoods were wealthy, then Antonia was determined that they should not believe that financially she was in their class.

Robert said immediately, "I'll come with you, Antonia."

She began to protest. "It's only a short distance—" But something in Cleo's upward-tilted, smiling face prevented her from further objection.

When they were outside in the street where Antonia lived, she said, "She's very pretty, your cousin."

"Oh, Cleo?" Robert answered. "Yes, she is, but she exploits her looks rather shamefully. She thinks she has only to bat her eyelashes at every man she meets and they'll fall at her feet. And most of them do."

Antonia laughed. "You sound dismal! She's only young and she knows it's very exciting to have a certain power and be able to use it."

"She's twenty," returned Robert, "and all I can hope is that she's going to grow up in the next year or so, because I want to marry her."

Antonia gave him a swift sideways glance. "Oh, I see."

"Actually, we're not first cousins," he told her, "but there's a distant and complicated relationship. It's so much easier to say we're cousins."

He left her at the door of the Albergo Violetta and Antonia went up to her room in a thoughtful state of mind. She wondered now if Robert was making his own position clear and distinct to her, that he and Cleo might be engaged, so that she did not mistake friendly help for a deeper interest. Well, perhaps it was all to the good to know exactly where one stood in these matters. Robert was attractive, kind and thoughtful, but she had taken his friendship in the spirit in which she believed it had been offered. It had not occurred to her to fall in love with him. She knew that his father owned a dozen companies connected with hotels, catering and department stores. Robert was

21

merely pleasing himself in working in Italy for a year.

The situation was underlined a day or two later when Cleo telephoned inviting Antonia to the Margharita for aperitifs at half past six.

"My Italian class doesn't finish until nearly six," explained Antonia, "but I'll be there as soon as I can. Thank you."

Cleo in a white lace dress over a blue foundation looked angelically luscious. Mrs. Norwood, by accident or design, provided the sharp contrast of a simply cut black shift, a diamond shoulder brooch the sole ornament.

Antonia decided on a plain vermouth, but Cleo declared she wanted to try a Negroni, that potent cocktail of gin, vermouth, Campari bitters and a slice of orange.

"Risky?" queried her mother.

"Not in moderation, I hope," was Cleo's smooth answer.

Mrs. Norwood was charming, but Antonia realised how skilful were the questions sandwiched between the small talk. Antonia, seeing no reason to hide or disguise the truth, gave frank answers.

"But if you stay here in Perugia too long, you won't see much of the rest of Italy," remarked Mrs. Norwood.

"Oh, I shall move on when I want to," Antonia answered. "I'm undecided at present." She was remembering that she had not yet made up her mind about joining Talbot Drury's expedition. She had not even written home to Philip, yet she must decide soon, for Talbot would need to know definitely.

Presently Mrs. Norwood excused herself, saying that she had a telephone call to make. Almost instantly Cleo's languid manner vanished.

"What happens when you finish your Italian course?" she asked, almost urgently.

Antonia's grey eyes widened. "I don't know."

"You'll stay here and paint?"

"Probably. I'd like to stay for a while if I could find a studio or share one with another painter."

"Robert's helped you a great deal, hasn't he?" pursued Cleo.

"Oh, indeed he has. He suggested the Italian course, then he arranged the exhibition for me. I've only drawings in that, of course. I hadn't any paintings ready, but—"

Cleo smiled and seemed to recover her former poise. "You do understand, of course, how things stand between Robert and me?"

"He told me after you arrived."

Cleo finished her drink and set down the glass. "Only then?"

"Does it matter when he told me?" asked Antonia.

"It might. Robert is so wonderfully attractive—"

"There's really no need to warn me, Cleo. I may call you that? I'm quite conscious of the fact that I've been given a wonderful opportunity to travel. I'm not going to waste it by falling in love with Robert—or, indeed, anyone else."

Cleo's face assumed a kindly, almost elder-sister expression. "You understand that I just don't want you to be hurt."

"Nothing to worry about," Antonia assured her with a geniality that she did not feel. Inwardly she was nettled by the patronising manner in which Cleo had warned her off. "Whether you and your mother are staying here or not, I doubt if I shall see much of Robert during the next few weeks." In her desire to appear offhand and casual, Antonia went much further than she had intended and her next words surprised even herself. "Apart from Italian lessons and painting, I've been asked to join Mr. Drury's archaeological team, so I shall have little time to spare."

Cleo's mouth rounded into a surprised "Oh!", then she glanced upward.

"I'm glad to hear that you've apparently decided to join us." A voice from behind Antonia's chair made her jump as she twisted round to see the speaker.

"You've heard from your godfather that he has no objections?" continued Talbot Drury.

"I—er—that is—well—" Antonia began incoherently, then became aware of Cleo's quizzical gaze. "Yes, I have decided, if you think I can be of use," she said emphatically, burning her boats conclusively. She was furious with herself that she had been foolishly provoked into a split-second decision before she had considered all the implications, before even she had actually written to Philip, let alone received his answer, encouraging or otherwise.

"Then perhaps we can go somewhere and discuss the details over a meal," suggested Talbot.

Antonia rose immediately, aware that no smile lingered on Cleo's face as Talbot bade her goodnight.

In the restaurant to which Talbot took her for dinner. Antonia honestly confessed that she had not yet mentioned the matter to Philip, her godfather, but would do so immediately.

"Why didn't you say so?" he asked testily. "Weren't you interested enough to do that?"

"I wanted time to think."

"And now you've thought—or have other circumstances made up your own mind for you?"

"If you mean that I see the position with Robert differently now that his girl friend Cleo has arrived, then you're quite wrong in your assessment of me." Her tone was as resentful as his, and suddenly his cold blue eyes warmed, almost twinkled as he looked across the table at her.

"I hope your godfather isn't going to prove an obstacle," he said. "I think we might find you quite useful on the site."

He, too, sounded patronising, but she wondered if she was now becoming too touchy. She listened carefully while he outlined the initial stages of the "dig".

"Some preliminary work has already been done, but we're not yet down to the interesting level, although even that is often uncertain. The hill-towns were built in all sorts of haphazard ways, so you don't know what you'll find at an impossibly superficial level."

"I could probably come to the site at week-ends for the time being," she offered.

He nodded absently. "I'll get in touch with you if it's necessary."

When he saw her to the Albergo Violetta, she had promised to write immediately to her godfather.

"I'll write tonight before I go to bed," she assured him.

In her room, she stared thoughtfully at the half-written letter to Philip. She hardly knew what answer to hope for. If he disapproved of her spending too long in one place, then she would be released from a rash and impulsive decision. If he raised no objections, then she would have to make the best of her own reckless-ness. What twist of timing had brought Talbot Drury close enough tonight to hear those words of bravado? Antonia wondered what she might have let herself in for, but underneath her hesitancy was the desire to stay as long as possible in Perugia, a magic city that fascinated her and seemed loth to let her go.

CHAPTER TWO

FOR most of a fortnight Antonia saw little of her English friends. Her life was bounded by the intensive course at the Unversity, with occasional evenings spent in the company of Ingrid and Sven, the two Scandin-avians; during most of the week-ends she painted in the hope that she might have something worth while to show to Robert's artist friend in due course.

She had heard from Philip and his letter had de-lighted her.

"Seize opportunities as they come," he had written, "that's a good reason for being young. Time is not wasted if you're absorbed in doing something, however futile it may appear later. Later on, perhaps, I might come to Perugia and see what goes on at one of these 'digs' . . ."

When she telephoned Talbot Drury that she had received most positive confirmation that Philip approved, Talbot's manner was unaccountably cool, even abrupt.

"We shan't need you for a couple of weeks yet," he had said. "I'll let you know later when to come to the site."

Antonia replaced the telephone receiver, puzzled and rather chilled. Perhaps Talbot was also regretting his offer. If so, she was now more determined to prove to him that she could be of use and not a hindrance.

When it came to Saturday, she decided to use her free time in visiting the excavation site for herself. The bus to Gubbio would take her in the right direction.

She pushed her way into the crowded bus and was lucky to secure a window seat, but now she almost regretted taking what might be a difficult and unnecessary journey, for the scene through which she passed was guaranteed to excite anyone who had an eye for beauty, much less one like Antonia who was trying to acquire the painter's vision.

Each turn of the road gave glimpses of villages with russet rooftops clustered about a pointed steeple, pink-washed houses were circled by the silvery blue-grey olive trees. Sometimes a belt of black cypresses cut across the land, punctuating the pastel colours with sharp contrast. Everywhere was the clear luminous light that the old Umbrian painters had captured in their landscape backbrounds. Antonia almost ached to leave the bus, put up an easel and reach for her brushes, but today she had come empty-handed and with a different purpose in mind.

She alighted at the road junction which Talbot had told her about and walked down the narrow road to the south. The sun became hotter and she missed the cool breeze so constant in Perugia. After more than an hour's walk, she wondered if she had missed the way.

She sat down on a convenient rock by the roadside to rest. Far away down the road she could hear the rattle of a truck. She could ask the driver if she was going the right way. At least she knew enough Italian for that. But the truck was driven at breakneck speed and covered her in dust as it passed. Then she heard the squeal of brakes and when she had wiped the dust from her eyes, she saw a man coming towards her.

When he came nearer she saw that he was Stefano, Talbot's assistant. He smiled, gave her a hearty *"Buon giorno, signorina"* but only then realised who she was. "Ah, the Signorina Meade!" he exclaimed.

Antonia explained that she was trying to visit the excavation site.

"But it is quite far," he said. His English was good, even if sometimes slightly fractured. "It is not for walking. I will ride you in the truck."

She was glad of his offer, although amused that he had not recognised her as he drove past, but was yet unable to resist the opportunity of picking up a girl by the roadside.

In the narrow lane he had to go some distance before he could turn and drive back to the site. He landed her at the edge of a cleared space of soil, pointed vaguely in the direction of a group of men, then drove off again the way he had come.

Antonia gazed about the site, noting that it was marked out in small numbered rectangles. A gang of a dozen or so men, stripped to the waist, shovelled earth into neat ridges on the edge of narrow trenches. She skirted the edge of the field, unsure whether Talbot was here or not. Then she saw him, talking to an Italian. He waved to her, then gave his attention again to his companion. After a few minutes he came towards her.

"What on earth are you doing here?" he demanded. "How did you come?"

"By bus, my own feet and Stefano's truck," she answered.

He gave an exclamation of impatience. "If only

you'd said you wanted to come, we could have fixed up transport. Don't be so crazy again."

It was a fine welcome, she thought, when she had taken the trouble to be interested enough to see what was going on.

Evidently Talbot was not aware of his brusque manner. "Well, now that you're here, you'd better come along with me and get the general idea of the layout," he said slightly less grudgingly.

He took her on a tour of the part that was being prepared. "We've only scratched the surface, so far," he explained, "but we don't know how far down we have to go."

Presently, as she stepped over pegs and sometimes white-painted lines marking the sections, he asked, "Brought your sketchbook with you?"

His tone implied derision.

"No," she replied evenly. "Only my lunch. I didn't imagine that a restaurant would be available here or even a simple *trattoria*."

He turned to glance at her and the ghost of a smile curved his lips. "Very sensible," he commented. "Are you ready to eat now?"

"Yes, I suppose so, if by that you mean you want to get rid of me as soon as possible."

"Over-ready to take offence where none is intended," he remarked to the distant view. "Come on, then."

He led her to a rough shack at the edge of the site. Spades, hoes, trowels and other tools were piled up outside. He manipulated a couple of stout poles and pulled out a rough awning that provided a patch of shade.

"The men use the inside of the hut for their meals, but I don't intrude on their free time." He hauled a wooden box from a pile and set it down. "I'm afraid we can't provide comfortable chairs. Will you put up with a box to sit on?"

"Of course," she said quickly. The top of the box was obviously dusty, but she was not going to appear pernickety and give Talbot the satisfaction of thinking her unsuited to working on a rough site.

To her surprise, he flicked the box quickly with a rag, before inviting her to sit. He sat on the dusty ground beside her and produced his own package of food, together with a bottle of wine.

"Try this," he suggested, handing her a small tumblerful. "It's a local wine from Lake Trasimeno."

She sipped it appreciatively. "How did you manage to keep it so cool?"

His blue eyes gleamed with amusement. "I've had to learn these small tricks, usually from the workmen on the sites. This bottle was wrapped in wet sacking, dumped into a zinc container full of ice. The advantage is that afterwards we can suck the ice."

She laughed spontaneously. "Economical, too. I can imagine that most of your work is very dusty and thirst-making."

She had brought only a small lunch, just enough cheese and salami and fruit to keep her going until the afternoon, but Talbot had some delicious cold trout which he shared with her, as well as portions of suckling pig and some very luscious little cakes full of fruit.

When she sampled them all, she said, "You've no intention of starving on the job, I see."

"If I'd known you were coming, I'd have provided more of the local specialities."

When they had finished eating and the bottle of wine was empty, he began to tell her why he had chosen this particular hillside for his excavations.

"Most of the ground between Perugia and Assisi has been fairly thoroughly worked over from time to time, but it occurred to me that there might be more interesting finds on this side."

"Have there been excavations here recently?" she asked.

"Not in this exact spot, but fairly near, and the results are in the museums at Florence and Rome." He sighed before he continued. "The trouble is that like all these old civilisations, there's been so much war and fighting and destructon that it's almost accidental if you find anything at all. One conqueror destroys the buildings of his enemies, builds his own on top and, in turn, they, too, are destroyed."

"So, if it were possible and you could look in the right place, you could go down deep enough to find whole Etruscan cities?" Antonia queried.

He smiled. "Fragments, perhaps. Too many layers, Roman, medieval, modern buildings and their ruins lie on top."

"But I read recently that only four or five years ago, bulldozers were clearing a site in the Perugian suburbs for new housing when they came across a wall and an Etruscan tomb."

He gave her a quick smile. "So you've been reading up Perugia? Yes, it was a good find. The pity is that so much good archaeological material is destroyed for ever when the bulldozers come on the scene, unless there is someone handy to identify what might lead to an interesting discovery."

When he was silent, Antonia's thoughts roamed over the conjecture that here where she was actually sitting now, a mysterious race of people had inhabited the hills and valleys, tilled the fields, made pottery, built their houses and finally furnished their tombs with works of art.

"And all of it was two thousand five hundred years ago," she murmured aloud.

But Talbot was now out of earshot and collecting tools. When he returned he asked, "D'you want to stay here? There's nothing very interesting going on at the moment. Transport is rather a difficulty, but Stefano could take you back to Perugia."

She hesitated. She could see now that, unprepared for her sudden visit, Talbot was finding her an embarrassment. Yet she was not particularly anxious to be driving alone with Stefano. Or had she misjudged this lively Italian with a flirtatious gleam in his eye? Undoubtedly Talbot would not suggest Stefano if he was not reasonably trustworthy.

Antonia made up her mind. "Thank you. Perhaps I'd better return to Perugia if you can spare Stefano."

"Good. I'll be getting in touch with you soon," Talbot promised. "Either direct at your hotel or through Robert."

He walked with her to the place where several trucks and lorries were parked, but she was surprised when Stefano led the way to a car, evidently Talbot's. She had imagined he would be taking the same truck in which he had given her a lift. It was too late to back out now without in effect accusing Stefano of designs of which he might be entirely innocent.

Talbot waved goodbye as though relieved to be rid of her and Antonia entered the car. Yet the Italian behaved impeccably, maintaining a lively chatter as he drove. He took her to the Hotel Margharita, evidently under the impression that she was staying there, and she did not correct him. When he handed her out of the car as though she were a duchess, he said, "It would give me very much of pleasure if you would accompany me to Città della Domenica one time. Perhaps tomorrow?"

"Oh, the place they call 'Sunday City?' I couldn't go tomorrow, I must work on my paintings."

He shrugged. "Then perhaps another Sunday?"

"Maybe," she agreed, not wanting to give him a flat "No."

She moved slowly into the courtyard of the Margharita, then when she was sure Stefano had driven off, she walked out again quickly and returned to her small inn.

After a shower, she changed her dress and went out to the Ricciotto restaurant where she had found good food at inexpensive prices. Here she was joined later by her two Scandinavian friends, Ingrid and Sven.

She mentioned that she had been out to the excavation site where Mr. Drury was working.

Ingrid wrinkled her pretty noise. "Digging in the dust is not for me," she said. "I am content to see what is here now. Today we have been to Assisi."

"Yes, I must go there again. There's so much to see," Antonia replied.

"Tomorrow we shall go to 'Sunday City,' " Sven said. "Will you come with us?"

Antonia hesitated, then laughed. "This is the second time today I've been asked to go there."

Ingrid waved her long white arm in a large gesture. "Oh, then in that case, we will let you go with your escort and perhaps we shall meet you there."

Antonia was instantly filled with mild alarm. "Oh, no, indeed. I would much rather come with you, if I may, even though it makes a party of three. You see, I declined the first offer."

Ingrid leaned back in her chair and laughed. "Of course you were invited by a charming and handsome Italian."

Antonia nodded. "I'll wait until I know him better before I accept his casual invitations."

"Sunday City," a pleasure park on the outskirts of Perugia, had only recently been built as an attraction for children and grown-ups, and on her visit next day Antonia was enchanted with its amusing variety.

With her friends, Ingrid and Sven, she rode on the miniature railway through Disneyland villages, past a swan lake, little zoos of live animals and grotesque carvings of petrified ones. Children were delighted to climb up into Tarzan's house high in a tree, peer inside the house of Snow White and the seven dwarfs or roam around the wigwams of the Indian village. Cafés and restaurants were placed at strategic points and there were several ballrooms.

Yet the local flavour of Perugia and its history had not been forgotten.

"Look at these monstrosities!" Antonia exclaimed, as Ingrid and Sven followed her into the archaeological "zone" dotted with ludicrous sculptures of Aztec and pagan heads and an elephant with colossal trunk and ears that came halfway down his body.

"That elephant must have been one of Hannibal's that escaped," she said to Ingrid.

At the main entrance stood a Tower of Babel and near by, a pair of twin columns, those tall rectangular towers that once served as fortresses and dwelling-places all over the provinces of Umbria and Tuscany.

When they were tired of walking about, the three companions went to one of the cafés, and as they sat at a table in the shade of an awning, Antonia noticed Stefano passing by with a dark-eyed Italian girl, her arm linked in his.

Antonia was inwardly amused. Stefano evidently had no scarcity of girl friends willing to accompany him on Sundays. She hoped he would not notice her, but suddenly his gaze swung in her direction and immediately he came across to her table, bringing his companion with him.

"Ah, so the *signorina* is here after all!" he greeted her in English.

Antonia introduced her Scandinavian friends, Stefano introduced Giulietta who gave Antonia several watchful glances when the conversation continued in English. Then the Italian girl gave Stefano's arm several discreet little tugs.

"Perhaps we shall see you in the dancing tonight," murmured Stefano as he allowed himself to be gently shepherded away.

Antonia smiled, but made no other reply than calling *"Arrivederci."*

As the Italian couple walked away, Stefano suddenly darted back to say quietly to Antonia, "The boss is here, too, with a lovely blonde."

Was there a hint of malice in his dark eyes as he gave Antonia this information? She could not be sure, but it seemed that he was relishing the double satisfaction of reminding her that she could have had his company today and warning her that the "boss" had his chosen companion.

She wondered idly who was the "lovely blonde," but wasted no more time in speculation, for there were still further attractions to visit, the archway fashioned in the shape of a grotesque mouth through which one could walk, the castle in the woods, the windmill, and finally the belvedere from which vantage point could be seen the valleys with vineyards and silvery olive groves, the pink-white mass of Perugia and, far away, other towns guarding the hilltops.

When the dancing began, Sven suggested they should visit the ballroom, but Antonia was reluctant, realising that three is an awkward number for dancing.

Sven said immediately, "Why should I not have two partners?"

"All right, I'll come for a while," Antonia agreed, feeling that she was more nuisance if she argued than if she accompanied Sven and Ingrid.

As the three ambled slowly alongside the lake with gliding swans and an artificial whale blowing a small fountain in the air, Antonia came face to face with Cleo and Talbot.

Cleo would have passed on with no more than a brief nod of acknowledgement, but Talbot stopped in front of Antonia.

"I'd no idea you'd be here," he said.

She smiled. " 'Sunday City' is for Sundays, I suppose? Let me introduce my friends."

The greetings over, Talbot said, "Were you thinking of dancing? We could make up a party, I suppose?"

A party of five? thought Antonia. She was certainly odd girl out today.

Before Ingrid or Antonia could answer, Cleo claimed that there was a great deal of the amusement park that she wished to see.

"We haven't seen half of it yet," she said, querulously.

Talbot looked from one girl to the other, then gave a resigned shrug. "Of course, Cleo, but I thought—"

"Oh, I'm not tired yet," she put in.

When she and Talbot had moved away in the opposite direction, Ingrid giggled.

"Antonia, you must be a very dangerous girl!" she said when at last she could speak.

"Dangerous? Why?"

"Because all the men's girl-friends drag the men away before you can attach them to you. First, there was the handsome Italian—no doubt it was he who asked you to come here today. Now it is the Englishman."

"As far as Mr. Drury is concerned," replied Antonia, "Cleo is not really his girl-friend. She's practically engaged to the assistant manager of the Hotel Margharita. She and her mother are staying there. I expect Talbot accompanied her because Robert was on duty at the hotel."

Privately, Antonia thought that Cleo had lost little time in annexing Talbot as a partner when he was available and Robert was not.

The three stayed an hour or so in the ballroom, Ingrid and Antonia most amicably sharing Sven as a dancing partner, then took the bus home after fiery rockets soared against the dark blue sky and cascades of coloured stars fell in graceful arcs.

Robert telephoned Antonia the next evening at the time he guessed she would have returned to the *albergo*.

"I've news for you," he said, "My friend Vittorio, the art expert, will be in Perugia on Wednesday and is willing to look at whatever paintings you have."

"Splendid! Not that I've done much more to them," she added, feeling guilty at having idled over the whole week-end.

"All the same, he'll look at them. But you must be prepared for frank criticism. He won't butter you up and he's not easy to please, but his advice is usually sound."

"Thank you, Robert. It's very good of you to take so much trouble for me."

"How did you like 'Sunday City' yesterday?" he asked.

"Oh, you know about that."

"Yes. Talbot mentioned that he had seen you there."

Evidently not Cleo. Did Robert not know that Cleo had been there too, with Talbot?

"I enjoyed it immensely," she said hastily. "Amusing and witty and quite unlike any other amusement park I've ever seen." She changed the conversation back to the paintings. "Where will your friend look at my daubs?"

"M'm, yes," muttered Robert. "Now where? I think you'd better bring them here by taxi on Wednesday evening. I'll find some properly-lit rooms here where you can show them to Vittorio."

On Wednesday she could hardly pay attention to her Italian verbs and tenses at the University. She was keyed up to such a pitch of excitement by the evening when she stepped out of the taxi outside the Margharita that she knew there would be a frightful anticlimax. She carried her canvases, two at a time, and put them in the service lift where Robert had directed her.

"They won't be disturbed by the hotel residents there and we can take them all up together."

Vittorio proved to be a tallish, plump Italian with expressive hands, smooth black hair and a mobile mouth which more or less indicated his critical appraisals.

"No. No," he pronounced, shaking his head and drawing in his lips in an expression that Antonio knew meant she had failed. "You have not caught the light. It must be luminous. That is the quality, the brilliance, that the old Umbrian painters captured. It is the wide space between hills and valleys."

"Thank you," murmured Antonia in a low voice. "I must try to do better." But in that moment she despaired of ever being a first-class painter.

"Now this robe," he continued, pointing to a canvas where she had copied part of *The Adoration of the Magi*, "this is not bad. You have depth and colour. But the landscapes must have light. Otherwise they do not belong here to Umbria, but perhaps to your own country where it is cloudy and more subdued."

"Yes, I understand," she answered, seeing her work now as the muddy, lifeless daubs they really were.

He had moved away from the oil paintings and was examining the drawings that had been on exhibition in the small studio a week or two ago.

"These!" he exclaimed. "They are also yours?"

She nodded.

"But one or two are very good. You can draw if you cannot yet paint."

Her spirits lifted on a wave of enthusiasm. "Perhaps the subjects were here ready to hand."

He picked up the one she had done of the Etruscan Gate, compared it with another showing part of the outside pulpit attached to the Cathedral.

He scrutinised other drawings, then moulded his lips into an expression of approval, nodded his head at the two still in his hand. "These I will take if they are for sale. What is your price?"

Antonia was so overwhelmed by the fact that someone, and a knowledgeable expert at that, actually wanted to *buy* her work that she could only flush and stammer that she had no idea of price.

Robert who had remained silent until now, said, "Signor Vittorio will make a fair deal with you, Antonia. Leave it to him this time. Next time you can start to bargain with him." He smiled encouragingly at her.

"With pleasure," she answered. "I'm glad to accept your offer."

Vittorio named a sum of lire which sounded very agreeable to Antonia, but became considerably diminished when she worked it out later in sterling. On the other hand she was so pleased at having made a sale that she would almost have given Vittorio the drawings for nothing in return for his commendation.

She thanked him for his advice. "I promise I'll try to work hard at the oils."

Robert helped her to stack the canvases. "We'll leave them here for the time being until after dinner. I've arranged for you to dine here with Cleo and her mother. Is that all right with you?"

"Fine," she said, appreciating Robert's thoughtfulness, but wondering how Cleo would take it.

To Antonia's surprise, Talbot was also at the same table. Apparently he was now taking most of his meals with the two Norwoods.

After dealing with the paintings, Antonia had of course tidied herself, but against Mrs. Norwood's exquisite grooming and Cleo's immaculate fairness, she felt grubby in her own dark blue linen.

She had not intended to refer to Vittorio's criticisms of her paintings, but Talbot asked, "What did the expert think of your work?"

Antonia smiled. "I expect he thought a good deal worse of them than he actually said. He was very kind and pointed out the faults most helpfully."

Cleo's gaze veered towards Antonia. "I should like to take up painting," she said. "But I wouldn't want to do ordinary landscapes or still life or stuff like that. I'd rather do abstracts. So much easier."

Antonia's dark eyebrows lifted. "Easier?" she echoed. "Many people believe that you have only to draw a few odd shapes, splash colour in where the fancy takes the brush and you have an abstract, but it isn't quite as simple as that."

"The art expert didn't buy any of your paintings, then?" Cleo queried.

"No," Antonia admitted immediately, "but that wasn't his function. He's not just a dealer."

"What did he think of your drawings?" asked Talbot.

"He said they weren't bad."

"But not good enough to sell?" pursued Cleo, evidently determined to reduce Antonia to the status of a bad amateur.

Antonia paused before replying, hoping that perhaps Mrs. Norwood would steer the conversation into other channels.

"What did he buy?" asked Talbot, translating Antonia's hesitation correctly.

"Only two. The Etruscan Gate and the pulpit outside the Cathedral," Antonia now answered quietly.

Talbot muttered an exclamation. "The Gate and the Pulpit—your two best drawings in the exhibition! I hope he paid you well for them."

Antonia smiled. "I counted myself lucky that he wanted to pay at all for them. No one wanted them in the exhibition."

"I wouldn't have minded having those," Talbot remarked.

"Well, Antonia can always go and do two more for you," put in Cleo. "Those old bits of architecture are always there. You've only to copy them."

In a way, Antonia was glad when the meal was over, the coffee served, for in a few minutes she could make her excuses and leave this trio. She did not much care for Cleo's patronising manner towards herself and she was irritated by the girl's provocative glances and smiles in Talbot's direction. Perhaps, even more, she was scornfully amused by his attitude to Cleo, bending his head attentively to listen to her prattling, behaving in an ultra-polite way to Mrs. Norwood. She would have thought that a dedicated archaeologist would have had more serious matters to consider than playing the male escort to a pretty girl and her elegant mother, especially when he knew the situation between Cleo and Robert.

However, it was none of her business, Antonia decided, and she was about to rise and make her round of thanks and goodbyes when Cleo jumped up, exclaiming, "Come on, Talbot! Look at the time!"

Talbot rose more slowly, while Cleo pecked her mother's cheek, called a breezy "goodbye," thrust her hand around Talbot's elbow and almost literally dragged him out of the hotel courtyard and thence into the street.

Antonia waited a moment or two, then said, "I must go, too, Mrs. Norwood. Thank you for letting me have dinner with you."

But Mrs. Norwood's face wore a slightly absent expression. When she turned back to Antonia, she said apologetically, "I'm so sorry, my dear. What were you saying?"

Antonia repeated that she must go.

"Yes, of course," replied the older woman. "I understand. Now I wonder where those two have gone in such a hurry. D'you know, by any chance?"

"No, I don't."

Mrs. Norwood smiled. "Perhaps it's the theatre, although if the play is in Italian I don't know what Cleo will make of it."

As Antonia crossed the courtyard, Robert appeared.

"Pleased about your first sale?" he queried.

"Delighted. Thanks to you, Robert. I'm grateful. Also, I feel I've passed a milestone with the good criticism your friend gave me. I'll collect my paintings and the other drawings and take them back to the *albergo*."

"They're all stacked ready for you, but I'll help you with them later. I must just have a word with Mrs. Norwood."

Antonia paused while he took one of the vacant chairs opposite Cleo's mother.

"Cleo not here?" Antonia heard him say.

Mrs. Norwood gave him a dazzling smile. "No. She asked you to excuse her. She and Talbot have gone to look at some arch or other that he wanted to show her at a certain moment when the sun shines on it or through it or something."

Antonia felt the muscles of her face tauten. It was obvious that Mrs. Norwood had no idea where Cleo and Talbot had gone out for the evening, but instead of guessing the theatre, she had cleverly covered up for Cleo by putting the onus of invitation on Talbot.

Antonia waited no longer. The Norwoods, mother and daughter, were not her concern and no doubt Robert was well used to Cleo's unpredictable ways.

Outside the hotel, she asked a porter to fetch her a taxi and began again the job of stowing her paintings in the cab.

Robert came out just as she was taking the last two.

"Antonia!" he called. "Why didn't you wait for me to help you?"

"It didn't matter, Robert. They're not exactly a ton weight."

His brows were puckered. "Did Cleo tell you where she was going with Drury?"

Antonia shook her head. "No. They just went out."

In the taxi she waved to him, but noted how despondent his face had become. Surely he was not imagining that an archaeologist for ever poking about in ruined cities could snatch Cleo from him. It was hardly likely that the dainty Cleo would take an interest in broken pieces of pottery or unearthing tombs.

On Friday evening, when Antonia returned after dinner to the *albergo*, she received a message that Signor Drury had telephoned and would like her to ring him back.

"Could you come to the site at the week-end?" he asked when she was put through.

"Well—er—yes, I could—"

"You have other plans?" he said.

"I'd made arrangements to go to Assisi on Sunday," she answered.

"Oh, I'll take you there some other Sunday," he snapped. "If you could come on Saturday, there might be something you could do. We've begun to uncover one or two interesting finds."

"Then in that case I'll be glad to come," she replied, instantly infusing her voice with more enthusiasm in case he should think her interest had already waned.

"Right. I'll pick you up in the morning, pretty early, about seven o'clock, so be ready," he instructed.

"All right," she agreed. She replaced the receiver slowly.

He certainly didn't hesitate to give his orders when it suited him. Last week she had gone to the site of her own accord and he had scarcely veiled his impatience to be rid of her. Now when she had arranged a visit to Assisi with Ingrid and Sven, he commanded her at a moment's notice to spend the whole of Saturday and probably Sunday at the excavation site.

CHAPTER THREE

ANTONIA was ready next morning, dressed appropriately, she hoped, in maroon stretch slacks with a matching tuck-in shirt and a scarf to cover her hair. She found someone downstairs and asked for a pot of coffee, for she realised that she had no time for breakfast at her usual café round the corner.

Back on her balcony, she waited, scanning the street, and as soon as a car drew up outside the inn, she picked up the bag containing her sketch-block in its case, a bundle of pencils, and flew down the stairs to the inn entrance, almost falling over a maid sweeping the floor.

Talbot was standing by the open car door and when he saw Antonia he gave her a blank, unsmiling stare.

"*Buon giorno!*" she greeted him.

"*Buon giorno!*" he muttered in reply, still continuing to gaze at her.

She was momentarily disconcerted. "Is there something wrong? My clothes?"

He came suddenly out of his trance, if that was what it was, and said quickly, "No. Perfectly all right." He opened the rear door of the car for her. Then she saw that Stefano occupied the seat next to the driver's and he turned now and gave her a dazzling smile.

Talbot was already in and driving down the narrow street because it was impossible to turn here.

"Have you had breakfast?" he asked Antonia.

"Some coffee," she answered.

"We'll get something on the way," he assured her.

A few minutes later, Stefano alighted at a small snack-bar and emerged with a basket of food, bottles of wine, flasks of coffee, hot milk; he slung the basket in near Antonia's feet, as Talbot prepared to drive off again.

"There are some aerial photographs on the seat beside you, Antonia," Talbot told her. "You might study them. They'll help when we get to the site."

She did as he instructed and was fascinated by the contours in the land, the markings and patterns plainly seen even though the land had been ploughed and till-ed for centuries.

Each photograph was compass-marked and caption-ed with the time of day when it had been taken. Most were near sunrise or sunset and she saw at once that long shadows cast by the rising or setting sun naturally showed up the mounds and ridges.

There were various other photographs taken from ground level, in overlapping segments from a single viewpoint, so that put together they completed a circle of the scene.

"Those are the cat's-eye views," Talbot informed her, obviously watching her in his mirror.

"Cat's-eye?" she echoed.

"Yes. If you look down at a patterned carpet from your own height, you see the design, the different colours. But imagine that you're a cat looking at the same carpet. All you'd see is a blur of pattern."

"M'm. I see. Just as you have to go up to the top of the Eiffel Tower to see the pattern of the gardens below."

"It's one good thing that flying has given to archaeo-logists. We don't need to waste time on the wrong sites."

Antonia noticed several changes at the site since her first visit. On the edge of the working area a shady enclosure of canvas pulled around four stout poles and roofed with an awning had been erected.

"Between spells out in the open," Talbot told her, "you'll be able to rest in there in some privacy."

"Thank you. I expect I shall be glad of a patch of shade."

"Go with Stefano when he's ready, Antonia. He'll take photographs and point out the exact details for you to sketch, but you have to work quickly or the light changes."

She nodded her understanding.

Stefano, however, insisted on having his second breakfast before he started work. "Two moments it will take only," he explained, "and you, *signorina*, had better also eat with me."

"Be quick about it, the pair of you," growled Talbot. "I haven't brought you out here for an early morning picnic."

He strode off smartly to a distant corner of the marked-out plots where a group of workmen were gathering to start the day's tasks.

"It is perhaps too early in the day for him to be pleasant," observed Stefano to Antonia. "But eat rolls and drink coffee while you have the chance."

"Certainly I will." She was glad to have something to eat, but she and Stefano took little time about it and in a few minutes he led her towards the site where a deeper trench had been dug and wooden supports put in to prevent the sides caving in.

"Now, this is the part," he explained, indicating an area marked with small dabs of white paint. He took a long-handled flat whisk brush and gently smoothed away some of the surface earth.

"What does Mr. Drury believe is here?" she asked.

"Who knows? Could be a whole tomb or a city or perhaps only a pottery urn or an earring," Stefano replied, and she understood his caution.

He took several photographs with only the slanting sun for light, then attached his flash-gun and took several more.

"Flash is no use," he said, "for it makes all become flat. But now you must stand here and draw what you see."

Antonia stared. "But I don't see very much," she objected. "Nothing but a few wrinkles in the earth."

Stefano laughed. "These wrinkles are important. Draw them. Presently your eyes will see more. I have to leave you and go to the men now."

Left alone Antonia began to sketch to scale and gradually she found that, as Stefano had told her, her eyes began to translate the hollows and roughness into a shape, a pattern of light and shade. She scrapped the first drawing and began again, this time with more precision and accuracy.

She numbered successive drawings as Talbot had instructed, and included precise details of location and depth, so that a general picture of the site could be built up. Stefano had left her a compass, measuring tape and other odds and ends, although she noticed that a piece of paper with details was pegged to the side. These labels, she realised, would be reproduced in Stefano's photographs and thus provide a check.

When she believed that she could do no more drawings of this particular part, she scrambled out of the trench and found Stefano, who gave her a second similar job.

This time, however, she had to descend a short ladder into the trench and work by the light of a torch suspended from an iron tripod placed across the cavity.

"Please do not move the torch," he warned her, "for if you alter it the light will be different."

Antonia discovered this was easier said than done, for as she switched on the torch, it gyrated on its length of chain, but eventually she stilled it, although occasionally as she worked she banged her head against it and set it spinning again. "Lucky it's a black rubber one and not hard metal."

By midday she had produced a dozen drawings to show to Talbot and Stefano when the whistle blew for lunch.

"Like a factory!" she murmured. "Everything stops for lunch."

"The men need their long break in the middle of the day," observed Talbot, walking by her side towards the tent shelter. "Otherwise they get tired and, worse than that, careless. You'll find a wash-basin and water inside the tent," he added. "When you've washed the dirt and mud off your hands, let us know and we'll join you for lunch."

"Thank you," she said with gratitude. "I was thinking I'd have to scrape the worst off with a paper handkerchief."

"We can't provide luxury hotel mod. cons., but we do our best to remain reasonably civilised," Talbot returned, his eyes alight with a sparkle that contained a certain smugness.

"To match at least the standard of Etruscan civilisation in which you're so interested," she retorted.

Stefano unpacked the large food basket and set out the cold meats and salad on paper plates. There was plenty of wine, and although the two men drank theirs straight from the bottle, Stefano had included in the basket a small tough little glass which he refilled for Antonia so many times that she begged him to stop.

"I shall be seeing lines and humps where nothing of the sort exists," she protested. "My drawings will give you false impressions of wonderful finds!"

Stefano merely laughed and handed her some little sweet cakes to finish the meal. When she asked what they were called he replied, "Dead men's bones."

"Oh, no!" she exclaimed. "Not while we're actually on an excavation site."

Talbot joined in the laughter. "But that's true. That's exactly what their name is. Perugian specialities." When she still looked dubious, he continued, "Ask for them in the pastrycook's next time. You'll see."

She was convinced though that the two men were teasing her, but the cakes tasted delicious in spite of their macabre name.

After the meal Stefano disappeared, so that he could take his siesta with the men and sprawl comfortably.

Talbot spent some time looking at the drawings Antonia had made and she waited anxiously for his approval.

Finally he nodded. "Yes, these are quite helpful," was his verdict.

"What exactly are you looking for?" she asked.

He turned towards her and his gaze disconcerted her. "I'm not sure," he answered after a pause, "and even if I knew, it isn't always wise to tell everybody."

"I'm sorry," she mumbled, but there was no real apology in her tone. Even if he did not want to take her into his confidence, there was no need to give her such a slap in the face.

She had turned away from him, but she knew that he was watching her. After a pause, he said, "Tell Stefano to put two careful knife-workers on this plot. If you're interested enough you could watch them. Then you might find out what we're after."

He moved away from the tented shelter and Antonia stretched herself out as comfortably as possible on a piece of sacking laid over the bare earth. She rested, but did not sleep, for her thoughts milled around the complex personality that was Talbot Drury.

What harm could it do if she knew the object of his search? All she wanted was to be able to use her intelligence and justify her inclusion as the only feminine member of the party. It would serve Talbot right if she packed up her belongings right now and returned to Perugia. Let him find another artist to grub about in trenches and sketch incomprehensible patches of earth!

But when the shouts from the men indicated that they were ready to start work again, Antonia rose, left the tent and asked to which plot Stefano had gone. When she arrived she sat quietly, watching two Italians working delicately with knives, scraping away a few particles of earth at a time, then using fine paintbrushes to smooth the surface.

At intervals Stefano instructed her to sketch quickly the new positions of uncovered humps and bulges. A young Italian boy, dressed in blue jeans and a grey shirt, stood watching at the edge of the shallow trench. The men spoke to him occasionally, laughing and smiling, but the boy did not smile. Antonia heard him ask in Italian, "Who is the woman? Why is she there?"

One of the men answered that the *signorina* also was working.

Antonia looked at the boy and smiled, confirming in

her rather stiffly precise Italian that she was working and not there for pleasure.

At last the boy smiled. "But you will become dirty," he told her. "It is not for women to dig in the earth."

She understood and answered, "But I like doing it."

He gave her a scornful glance. "I would not let my sisters work so."

He turned his back on the group and walked away without further words.

"Does he live close by?" she asked one of the men.

"A small house on the hill. His father died a year ago, so he is head of his house now, and there is the mother and two sisters and two more small ones to look after."

Antonia raised her head. "What d'you mean? Look after?"

"He works to keep all his family," put in another man.

Antonia thought she had not understood the Italian phrases. "How old is he, then?"

The men shrugged. "Perhaps fourteen."

Antonia expressed her surprise. "How can a boy so young keep an entire family?"

"Luciano does it. He is very proud, you see. He is a Perugian."

As she bent her head to sketch a new portion of earth, she wondered if being a Perugian was adequate explanation that a young boy should have the entire responsibility of his family. She hoped the boy, Luciano would come again.

But when she arrived back in the tented shelter, which she privately dubbed "Agincourt," all thoughts of the boy were driven out of her head.

Reclining on a car rug and with Talbot's jacket for a pillow was Cleo.

"What on earth—" began Antonia.

Cleo sat up quickly, then subsided on to one elbow when she saw Antonia enter. "Oh, I thought it was Talbot," she said, yawning.

Antonia began to laugh. "Lolling there, you looked like your namesake, Cleopatra, in her barge drifting along the Nile when Antony first caught sight of her, although, of course, she had leopard skins to lie on and sweet music to beguile her."

"Is that meant to be funny?" asked Cleo crossly.

"Not particularly." In the first moments of leaving the bright sunshine outside and entering the shadowed interior of the tent, Antonia's attention had been focused by Cleo's mass of fair hair, but now she noticed Cleo's clothes—white shirt, khaki jodhpurs.

"Where's Talbot?" inquired Cleo.

"I don't know exactly. Somewhere about on the site." Antonia walked towards the corner where the washbasin and water jug stood on a packing case, but both were empty. "Oh! No water," she murmured.

"I was simply filthy by the time I arrived here," explained Cleo. "Isn't there any more?"

"Doesn't matter," replied Antonia, wiping her hands vigorously on a piece of rag. "Does Talbot know you're here?"

Cleo's smile blended triumph and disdain. "Naturally. He invited me. You don't think you're the only one to be useful in his work, do you? He told me that he'd be delighted if I'd come and help him."

"Oh, I see. What exactly are you going to do?"

"Same as you. I can sketch or take photographs. There's nothing much in that."

Antonia remained silent. She guessed that Cleo's interest in the site would soon wane. Excavations were something new to her. But Cleo's next words brought Antonia into sharp awareness of the situation.

"In a way, I'm rather glad you're here, too," continued Cleo, "or else I don't think my mother would have liked the idea of my being the only girl here among all these men." She gave a delicious little ripple of laughter. "So if you're here, I shall have a chaperone."

"Chaperone?" echoed Antonia, feeling suddenly that she had aged a quarter of a century in five minutes.

"Yes. Besides, it's not very correct for you to be here alone and no other women," Cleo pointed out.

"I hadn't thought of it," muttered Antonia. Immediately, she wanted to retract those words, even though they were true.

The look on Cleo's face said plainly that Antonia's attractions would never place her in such peril as Cleo's own glamorous appearance and personality.

Antonia smouldered with rage and resentment, not against Cleo who could hardly help her ravishing fairness, but against Talbot. He had known that he wanted Cleo's company at the site, but that her mother's permission might be difficult, so he had hurriedly telephoned Antonia, almost ordering her to give up her week-end.

Antonia moved out again into the sun just as Talbot and Stefano approached.

"Finished your drawings?" queried Talbot.

Without answering, Antonia picked up her sketch-block and handed it to him. Talbot and Stefano examined the successive pages.

"You haven't added the time of day to this one." Talbot pointed out.

She added a time halfway between the preceding drawing and the following one. "Does that satisfy you?" she asked.

He gave her a sharp glance, but by then she had half turned away. At the sound of men's voices, Cleo had come outside the tent. She leaned provocatively against one of the poles supporting the canvas surround and the awning, and Antonia longed uncharitably for the pole to give way and send Cleo subsiding into a heap. Even so, Cleo would enjoy being rescued by two men. As it was, Stefano was gazing at the girl in open-mouthed admiration.

"I came after all, as you see," Cleo said, obviously nettled that the two men did not immediately throw their business matters aside.

"Yes, so I see," agreed Talbot. He tore Antonia's

drawings from the sketch-block, which he handed back to her, then put the drawings into a folder.

"D'you want me to come tomorrow?" Antonia asked.

Talbot glanced at her. "I thought we'd arranged that. D'you want to do something else?"

"I might as well come here if I can be of help," she answered coolly.

"I shall be here tomorrow," Cleo put in, "so you must come, too. I'll bring you in my car."

Neat, thought Antonia. The "chaperone" idea was to be very obviously demonstrated. Additionally, it would ensure that Antonia would be Cleo's passenger instead of riding with Talbot. Perhaps that was for Robert's benefit.

"All right," agreed Antonia briskly. "Perhaps you could also drive me home when you're ready."

Cleo's face clouded. "Actually I'd arranged to take Talbot in my car—"

"Oh, no," he interrupted hastily. "I've still work to do here with Stefano. You two girls go home and we'll follow later."

Cleo was unused to being dismissed so decisively and her face revealed her surprise, but she recovered her casual expression. "I shall be ready in about half an hour, Antonia," she said, obviously hoping that during that time she would find an opportunity of diverting Talbot's attention to herself or that Antonia would grow tired of delay and find some other means of transport back to Perugia.

But Talbot and Stefano went to a distant corner of the site and Cleo had no choice but to lead the way to her car.

It was a comparatively silent journey and neither girl mentioned Talbot's name, however much he might be in their thoughts.

Antonia directed Cleo to the narrow street where the small inn was situated.

"So this is where you live?" queried Cleo. "Small place."

"It's quite comfortable and I have that room up there

with the balcony. Very pleasant," replied Antonia. "But of course, it doesn't compare with the Margharita or the Brufani Palazzo."

This innocuous remark seemed to annoy Cleo. "Naturally we'd be staying at the Brufani if Robert were not wasting his time at the Margharita."

"But surely you couldn't call it waste of time to be perfecting himself at his job," Antonia said mildly.

"Except that he doesn't need a job at all, but he's so obstinate and independent," retorted Cleo, slamming the car door. "I'll pick you up tomorrow about ten o'clock. 'Bye."

She had driven off down the narrow street before Antonia could protest that by ten o'clock half the early sunlight would have gone and Talbot would be displeased. Yet as she walked up to her room she reflected that perhaps after all Cleo had the right ideas. Why should one always dance to Talbot's tune? It might do him good to learn that people were not puppets leaping to his commands.

Robert telephoned later that evening that he had found a share of a studio for Antonia.

"It's only a small, poky little place, you understand," he explained, "but you might be able to work there better than in your bedroom."

"It will certainly make me more popular with the landlady here," replied Antonia enthusiastically. "What with the smell of oils and her constant fear that I'm going to daub the walls with dobs of raw sienna, she's in a state of nerves."

Robert laughed. "Painters are no new experience to her, I expect. What she really wants is a little more money for the privilege."

"Where is the studio?"

"Just off the Corso Garibaldi, not far from the San Angelo Gate. You'll be sharing with a girl named Francesca, so you'll be able to polish up your Italian with her."

"When d'you think I should go and see her?" querried Antonia.

"As soon as you like. I've arranged provisional payment, only a small amount which I think you can afford. Anyway, try it for a week or two. If you find it doesn't work out well, you can soon move your gear back to the *albergo*."

"Thank you, Robert, for fixing all this for me," she said. "I shall be able to work twice as fast now."

"Unless you're going to spend all your spare time on Talbot Drury's excavation site. Have they found anything interesting?"

"Not yet, I think," she replied cautiously. "They're hoping they may come on something soon."

After Robert's call, Antonia stood undecided. She longed to see this studio at the earliest moment, but there was little point in viewng it after dark, nor was it likely that Francesca would be there on a Saturday night. But if Cleo were not coming until ten o'clock tomorrow, there would be time to visit the studio earlier. She telephoned Cleo at her hotel, asking to be picked up by the Etruscan Gate instead of at the inn.

"I have a call to make near the Corso Garibaldi and I'll meet you at the gate sharp at ten. It's on the way to the site."

"Don't be late, then," advised Cleo, "or I might not wait."

Antonia laughed to herself. It was far more likely that Cleo would be unpunctual.

The studio turned out to be an attic room in a tall old house and Francesca was padding around in a dressing-gown when Antonia arrived next morning.

The Italian girl yawned sleepily as she showed Antonia over the large room with a sloping roof and a good north light.

"I do not speak much English," she said.

"We shall manage with your English and my Italian," prophesied Antonia gaily, sensing that she would get on well with this new friend. At this moment Francesca's pale, high-cheekboned face appeared apathetic, but Antonia guessed that when the other girl

53

was really wide awake, her dark eyes would sparkle, her mobile mouth curve in animation.

"I will pay you now for the first week," Antonia offered, placing a note in Francesca's hands. "Then we will settle later by the month, perhaps."

Francesca looked slightly blank and Antonia translated as best she could, adding in Italian, "Tomorrow I will bring my canvases and the rest."

Francesca nodded. "*Arrivederci*."

Antonia reached the Etruscan Gate a good quarter of an hour before Cleo was due and to while away the time she took out her sketch-block and began on a drawing from a different viewpoint. Engrossed in her task, she was unaware of time until a glance at her watch showed nearly half past ten. Had Cleo gone off without her, then? Had the message gone astray, or had she forgotten about the altered meeting-place?

Antonia decided to wait five more minutes, then go in search of a bus, but just them an impatient motor-horn signalled Cleo's arrival.

Antonia swung herself and her packages into the car.

"Did you bring a picnic lunch?" she asked Cleo.

"No. Should I have done?"

"All right. You can share mine. The men will provide us with wine," Antonia assured her.

"I thought we'd go off to some village inn close by and have a decent lunch," Cleo remarked.

"The site is some distance from any village. There are only a few scattered houses."

When the two girls arrived, Antonia left Cleo in the car and went off immediately in search of Talbot, but it was some time before she found him or Stefano.

"Good afternoon!" he greeted her. "I thought you'd decided not to come after all."

Before Antonia could frame a suitable reply, Cleo, who was close behind her, put in, "Antonia had some important call to make first and then she was busy sketching one of those old gates."

Antonia turned, a furious expression on her face. "But, Cleo, you——"

"Well, now you're here," interrupted Talbot, "I'd better start you on some job or other or else you'll blame me for wasting your time."

Antonia followed him in stony silence. It was clever of Cleo to put all the onus of their late arrival on to Antonia's shoulders.

She worked under Talbot's direction until the midday break for lunch, then accompanied him to the tent which everyone now called "Agincourt," although it became comically pronounced by some of the Italians. She offered some of her food to Cleo, who refused it in favour of delicacies from Talbot's provisions. When the meal was over Antonia unobtrusively moved away from the tent and rested outside with her head in the shade of a piece of planking she had erected between two or three heavy stones.

When it was time to start work again, Talbot spoke to her.

"Why are you sulking, Antonia?"

"I wasn't aware that I was."

"Perhaps you find working here less interesting than you thought it would be, then?" he queried.

"No. It's more interesting than I thought, providing I'm doing it for a real purpose and not just to be given a task to fill in the time." Her face was turned away into the shadow.

"What on earth d'you mean by that? Or am I supposed to answer riddles? Of course you're doing it for a real purpose. D'you think I'd clutter myself up with girls just to have them decorate the site?"

"No, I'm sure you wouldn't," she retorted. "Tell me what I'm to do next and I'll start."

His blue eyes shot her a penetrating glance. He pointed out the trench where he wanted the next set of drawings and she went towards it smartly, not looking back, but wholly aware that he was watching her.

At the end of the day, Antonia had forgotten her earlier irritations and was pleased when Talbot complimented her on her drawings.

"These are very helpful indeed," he said. She tried

not to believe that he was making an unusual effort to reassure her that her services were of value.

She wondered idly, as she brushed the dust and earth off her clothes, what Cleo had been doing all the afternoon. The girl was nowhere in evidence now.

"Has Cleo gone back?" she asked Talbot.

"I suppose so. I can give you transport back to Perugia."

Stefano had apparently gone earlier, too, for Talbot had no other passengers.

"Have you been to a town called Gubbio?" he asked Antonia when he was driving home. "It's a few miles farther up this road."

"No, not yet. I must make an effort to go there some time."

"There's a feast-day on next week. Quite interesting, I believe. I missed it when I was here before. 'Feast of the Candles,' they call it," he told her.

"Yes, I think I've read about it somewhere."

"It's on Wednesday. Would you like to go?"

She turned towards him. "I couldn't go in the daytime. I have my Italian classes."

He gave her a quick smile before turning his attention again to the winding road. "Oh, skip your classes for once. We could both take a day off and go to Gubbio together."

She paused a few moments before replying. "I suppose there's a museum there and you want me to make copies of drawings or exhibits?"

"I hadn't thought of that. But if you prefer to stew in the museum while the town has gone gay in holiday mood, you'll have your chance."

She laughed. "No, of course not." Then a new thought struck her. "Am I supposed to be chaperoning someone again?"

She saw him frown. "What on earth do you mean by that? Chaperoning?"

"Sorry. I thought perhaps I was being invited to accompany Cleo." Now that she had started on this subject, she had no choice but to continue.

"Cleo? Why should she come into it?" he demanded.

"Well, I thought that was why I'd been asked to come to the excavation site this week-end. Cleo made it clear that her mother was glad that I—rather, that there were two of us at the site."

Talbot gave a sigh that was more like a snort. "Oh, lord! I shall soon begin to wish I'd started digging in Mexico or Syria or somewhere else far removed from this part of Italy. It's always the same. One girl, fine. Two girls—anarchy!"

She remained silent, although she longed to ask him about his earlier experiences with one girl or two girls on the digging sites.

"Cleo invited herself," he continued. "I told her she could come at week-ends, provided she kept out of the way of the important spots. It's only curiosity. She'll soon get tired of the dust and discomfort."

"You can't blame me for wanting to know where I stand," she mumbled.

"And I can tell you equally where *I* stand," he retorted. "I'm here on a job of work that needs all the concentration I can give it. I've neither time nor inclination to waste my energies on squiring girls, especially one who, I understand, is about to be engaged to Robert."

"The other girl understands the situation perfectly," Antonia said smoothly.

"Are you now going to throw my offer of a day at Gubbio in my teeth?" he asked, an amused curve to his lips.

"You said you hadn't time for squiring girls," she reminded him.

"All right, then. Let's say that I'm asking one of my assistants to spend the day with me in an interesting town on a gala occasion." His tone was pomposity itself.

She began to laugh. "The assistant will be delighted to come, if I can square it with my Italian professor."

Antonia spent the next evening removing all her

painting gear from the inn to the studio, which she was to share with Francesca.

The Italian girl told Antonia, "You can sleep here if you come home late from a party, but not all the time."

Antonia thanked her. "Oh, I don't go to parties that keep late hours."

She was surprised to discover how impatient she was to visit Gubbio for the Feast of the Candles. She did not mention the event to Ingrid or Sven in case they suggested a threesome again and she had to make excuses that she already had a partner. At any rate, the festival was listed on the University notice board, so the calendar was there for anyone to read.

All the same, Antonia felt slightly guilty of petty meanness and as she stood surveying her small stock of dresses, she wondered why she wanted to keep the outing so secret. She pushed aside the thought that a day spent with Talbot Drury was an attraction in itself, regardless of festive occasions.

CHAPTER FOUR

TALBOT called for Antonia punctually at eight o'clock next morning as he had promised, and when she saw him dressed in fawn Terylene jacket and trousers, a white shirt and even a tie, she was glad that she had taken some trouble with her own appearance. She had chosen a hyacinth-blue Crimplene dress, aware that it accorded well with her grey eyes and brought out the bronzy lights in her hair. She carried a lacy white wool stole in case the evening might be cool.

"How fortunate that we men usually dress in more neutral colours," he remarked as she entered the car. "Think of it if I wore a suit of strawberry pink!"

She turned to meet his glance. "Pink is not your colour," she said decisively. "If you'd lived in medieval times or even later, you'd have been a peacock in royal blue velvet with magenta doublet, or later, you might have worn apple-green satin breeches and a coat of gold cloth embroidered in lavender."

He made a wry face. "Present day drabness has its merciful advantages. I suppose you're very erudite on the subject of historical costume?"

"It was included in my art training," she answered, "and I'm very interested in the subject because if I find out eventually that I'm never going to be a painter of more than mediocre talent, then I might try to amuse myself with theatrical design."

She told him that she now had a half-share in a small studio.

"So now, I suppose, all your week-ends are going to be spent painting?" he asked.

"Oh, no. I shall come to the excavations if you have work for me to do there."

He made no further comment, but after a pause began to tell her of the Feast of the Candles. "That's only a colloquial name for it. It's really the *Corsa dei Ceri*, the Race of the Wax Effigies."

"Not real candles at all?" she queried.

"They have those at night, but in the daytime they have these three effigies, massive constructions of wax, and teams of men haul them through the narrow streets, each section of the city trying to win the race. The best part, so I'm told, is at the finish in the main Piazza when teams that have had to plod behind the leading one make a dash for it as soon as they reach the square and sometimes win by a short head."

The streets were thronged with people in holiday mood and after Talbot had parked the car in a side street evidently not on the processional route, he guided Antonia towards the main streets and then to the beautiful Consul's Palace, a high building crenellated and turreted of warm amber stone, with pairs of arched windows and a massive doorway.

The wide steps were already filled with people ready for a good view of the procession when it passed, but Talbot took Antonia towards a small side door guarded by three officials. After a few brief words, the official nodded and smiled and pointed the way up a narrow staircase.

"We shall have a better view up here," Talbot told her as they mounted flight after flight until at last they emerged on to a roof-piazza, where some of the leading citizens were greeting each other. Long benches and additional chairs had been placed for spectators.

"Now you can see Gubbio's fine Roman amphi-theatre." He pointed to the curving arena only a field or two away just outside the town.

"I'd no idea it was so near," she said. "They use it, of course?"

"Naturally. Throughout the summer there are class-ical plays. Apart from the mausoleum, it's about all that remains of the old Roman city."

"No excavations going on here at present?" she asked.

"Most probably someone is poking about some-where around the outskirts of the town."

"When does the race start?" she asked after she and Talbot had walked round the roof admiring the views that opened out in every direction.

"At noon," he replied. "I've brought you up here rather early, but I guessed that if we left it later we might not even be able to get through the crowd down below."

She smiled at him. "And be ushered in through a secret side door? I take it you're a privileged person here."

"Not really," he disclaimed. "I wrote to the Mayor a few days ago and asked if I could have a rooftop view." He paused to give her an oblique glance. "Of course I discreetly added that I was working on a dig close by."

The noonday chime from the Cathedral was the sig-nal for the start of the race, and soon the mumurs from the packed crowds in the streets below roared to a crescendo as the leading team evidently came in sight.

Peering through the crenellated battlements, An-tonia caught a glimpse of about twenty men in bright

60

yellow shirts and white trousers, carrying a platform supporting a dark, candle-like shape some twenty feet high, with a curved waist about halfway up. The conical top held, in place of a wick, a golden figure with a flying cloak. Close behind came a second team dressed in dark blue shirts with black sashes, pulling a similar waxen construction with a different saint's figure on top. Almost on their heels came a third team wearing red shirts. Each team had a leader who walked in front, often turning to exhort his men to even greater efforts.

"Do they toss for positions?" Antonia asked, forced to shout to Talbot above the din of cheering crowds and a band playing lively marching airs.

"They draw lots, I believe, but it's a case of a quick start to get round the first corner into a street where the other teams can't pass."

"I see. Like our Boat Race. If you're nippy off the mark you can take the other side's advantage."

Even as she spoke and shifted her viewpoint, Blue Shirts closed into a narrow width, made a tremendous spurt and, urged on by the shouts and gestures of their leader, managed to scrape past Yellow Shirts as the processional route curved past the foot of the Consul's Palace. The crowds gave way, then surged forward again as the following Red Shirts tried to take a similar advantage, but civil police gently pushed back the spectators, which from Antonia's vantage point appeared no more than pygmies.

"Which team do you think will win?" she asked Talbot as he guided her to another part of the roof from where she could look down on a narrow street through which the first team would emerge.

"I'm not sure. Which one do you say?"

"I'm backing the Blue Shirts. Look how well they manoeuvred that corner."

"Right. My money's on Yellow Shirts. If you win, you shall have two pounds of the famous Perugina chocolates, your own selection."

"And if I lose?" Her grey eyes danced as she turned to look at him.

"I shall have to concentrate on what I can exact as forfeit." His gaze was directed at the distant hills outside the town, but there was a mischievous curve to his mouth. "Let's say a couple of cigars as a first instalment."

"Ah!" she sighed with mock gravity. "Nothing permanent. Chocolates to be enjoyed, cigars to vanish in smoke." Then as she realised the implications of her words, she blushed. She had made it sound as though she wanted him to give her presents of a more lasting, durable nature.

But now all attention was on the team emerging in the street below.

"Blue Shirts!" exclaimed Antonia, clapping her hands.

"With Yellow Shirts on their heels," put in Talbot. "The next corner may prove their advantage."

For a time the race disappeared from view and Talbot and Antonia joined the group of people clustered round the mayor and other distinguished citizens. A steward brought a tray of drinks and as Antonia and Talbot raised their glasses to their favoured teams, the mayor bustled forward to Talbot with welcoming greetings.

Talbot's Italian was rough-and-ready and Antonia noticed his grammatical errors, but she admired his fluency and when he introduced her to the mayor, she was glad to be able to respond to his salutations in his own language.

"Signorina Meade is studying at the Gallenga in Perugia," Talbot added.

The mayor expressed his good wishes for her success, but now the cheering and roaring in the streets below indicated that the Wax Effigies were nearing the finishing post.

With hurried bows and handshakes, the mayor and his friends dispersed to their special viewing stand and

Talbot and Antonia ran to the corner of the roof-piazza.

"Blue Shirts are leading!" she exclaimed excitedly.

"Yellow Shirts have not yet lost," he reminded her.

"What would happen to our bets if Red Shirts came up at a canter and won after all?" she asked.

"Null and void, as they say. You'd lose your chocolates and I my cigars, so you'd better not hope for an outsider's win."

Space had been cleared in the Piazza and the crowds pushed back so as to give fair chances to all teams to cross the line, but Blue Shirts, heaving and straining at their burden, their shoulders hunched under the horizontal poles that supported the effigy with its figure of a local saint on top, made a final spurt to win only a couple of yards in front of their competitors.

"Your chocolates are safe," Talbot mocked Antonia. "You shall have your winnings as soon as possible. But now for lunch."

Antonia thought with apprehension of the crowds in the streets and restaurants. With all these thousands of people milling about, would it be possible to be served anywhere?

When she and Talbot reached street level, he grasped her hand and tucked it within the crook of his elbow. She was a little surprised at this friendly gesture, although grateful for his forethought. She did not want to be lost in this happy holiday crowd.

When at last she and Talbot reached a restaurant on the corner of a quiet street, they entered a dark cavern-like passage that led to a vine-covered terrace.

The contrast between the excitement outside and this cool, peaceful oasis made Antonia sigh with appreciative contentment.

"How did you find such a delightfully quiet place?" she asked Talbot, who had been handed the menu.

"You've forgotten that I told you I was a mineralogist. I used my divining rods." He laughed. "No, I'll confess that I've been here several times and I ordered a table here today. Will you eat Umbrian food or international?"

"Oh, Umbrian, please," she replied quickly. "I hope I've left behind some of my insularity in England."

She enjoyed everything he ordered; the mountain lamb and black truffles, the special Perugian cheesecake, all accompanied by local wines. After a long leisurely lunch Antonia walked with Talbot through some of the streets of the town, quieter now while many of the visitors and townsfolk took a siesta after the excitement of the race and a substantial midday meal.

They walked as far as the Roman amphitheatre and sat on seats in the centre of a tier, conjuring up imaginary spectacles in the arena below.

"Would they have had gladiators here?" she asked.

"Probably, but mostly plays, I should think, and other entertainments. Circuses, perhaps. Up there is the Consul's own private box." He pointed out a structure with two arches and a flight of steps leading to it.

"Who occupies it in these days?" she queried.

"The mayor and his distinguished guests, no doubt."

When they moved to the topmost part of the amphitheatre, Antonia stood gazing at the town. "Yellow stone, old grey buildings, russet roofs—it looks like a medieval city painted in heraldic design," she murmured.

"I think it's kept its medieval character a good deal more than many other Italian cities. Through not being quite so large as Perugia, it hasn't attracted so many warring activities and destroyed itself with murderous feuds."

Talbot took her on a leisurely tour through the town, pointing out the various palaces and showing her the most distinctive features: the Renaissance courtyard of one, the beautiful façade of another.

"We must come another day and look at the famous Eugubine Tables in the Consul's Palace," he told her.

"What are they? I'm sorry to be so ignorant."

"Bronze tablets. Their importance lies in the fact that they contain directions for religious rites, written in Umbrian, Latin and Etruscan lettering. It's one of the very few examples which can throw any light on the Etruscan language or the Umbrian."

"What happened to these languages? Don't they even exist in dialect form now?"

"The Romans completely stamped out all forms of other languages," he replied.

While she was still pondering this tyrannical procedure, she and Talbot had arrived at a fountain in the centre of a square and she was astonished to see a procession of people madly circling the outside of the fountain basin.

"They seem to have enough energy to run round it, even after lunch," she commented.

"That's probably why it's called the Fountain of the Madmen. Come on, let's join them."

He seized her hand and almost before she knew what was happening he had pulled her into the gyrating mob.

"Why do we do this?" she panted breathlessly. "To prove that we're mad?"

His answer was to smile down at her and urge her to an even faster pace.

"Three times round and that's the lot," he said, when they broke away from the ring of laughing, shouting people. "Now you're a citizen of Gubbio."

When she recovered her breath a little, she laughed. "I don't wonder they call it the Madmen's Fountain. Is it really a tradition—this running round it—or are you kidding?"

"Kidding?" His features expressed exaggerated indignation. "Really, Miss Meade! D'you think I have so little respect for Italian customs that—"

"All right. Skip it," she interrupted. "I believe you. Now tell me what does citizenship of Gubbio mean to me? What can I do or have that other people can't?"

"Prestige of belonging to a beautiful medieval city,

that's all. How material you are! D'you think you get free ice-creams or something like that?"

She shook her head, laughing. The day was made for enjoyment and she was taking her full share of it. She had not realised until now what an excellent companion Talbot could be when he chose. He could make an old city come alive without the intrusive guidebook technique; he could forget his dignity and participate in giddy quixotic customs.

She hoped that nothing she did or said would spoil this happy holiday which she would always remember as the Feast of the Candles, although that was not even its correct name.

After dinner at a restaurant in the centre of the town, she and Talbot walked in the public gardens to admire the illuminations, the floodlighting and strings of coloured *lampadini* swaying in the breeze.

"There's one more procession to come," Talbot told her, "but we needn't watch it for long. We'll stay at one point and let it pass us."

The main streets were now lined with spectators waiting for the slow approach of the townsfolk, headed by church leaders. This time everyone carried tall candles as they chanted. Youth groups displayed painted structures of transparent material, boats, houses, castles, all lit from inside and many of the young people wore national or local costumes.

"This really is the Feast of the Candles," Antonia said.

After the procession, fireworks glowed and sparkled against the sky, showers of red stars and whirling streams of blue and gold fire.

"Are you tired yet?" Talbot asked Antonia, when they sat down to rest at a pavement cafe.

"Not if there's anything exciting to come," she answered, sensing that the evening had not yet ended, but that Talbot did not exactly want to wear her out with gaiety.

"There'll be dancing in the piazza," he told her.

She nodded. "Good. I can stand it if you can."

Under coloured floodlights a whirling mass of people jigged and jogged to the accompaniment of the town band, and Talbot and Antonia joined the edges of the crowd, but were soon engulfed. Pressed against him by the surrounding crush, she experienced a heady feeling which she refused to define. His nearness, his arm closely enfolding her in case she was torn away, the culminating excitements of the holiday, these things, she reasoned, all combined to kindle an exaggerated sense of magic in the air. She must keep her emotions under control. Dancing with Talbot Drury in this restricted space was no different from what it would have been if Robert or any other personable young man were her partner.

One must keep one's feet on the ground, she reflected, although that was difficult enough when so many times she was lifted off the ground to land on someone else's feet, usually Talbot's.

Gradually he worked his way again towards the edges of the crowd so that he and Antonia could take a breather.

In the general noise it was difficult to distinguish any particular voice, but Antonia fancied she heard someone call to Talbot. Suddenly she was standing alone and Talbot had disappeared. She gazed quickly about her, then found herself seized by a dark-haired man, but speedily disentangled herself from him and the rest of the dancers and walked across to the nearest building.

What on earth had happened? If I stand here fairly conspicuously, she argued, Talbot will be able to see me more easily. She scanned the heads that rose above the average, for he was taller than many of the Italians, and easier to distinguish because of his fair hair. Then she saw him and called out quickly, "Talbot! Talbot!"

She moved towards that part of the crowd. Then she saw that pressed against his white shirt was another fair head. Cleo's.

For a few moments she was stunned and remained

motionless until a group of laughing dancers gently swept her out of the way.

So this was what Talbot had been waiting for all day, all the evening, filling the time busily for himself as well as Antonia, giving her the impression that she was really his guest of the day, when he had probably arranged to meet Cleo here in the Piazza, but had wanted to avoid the appearance of discarding Antonia. What more natural than that a man should change partners easily in such a free-for-all in this open-air amusement?

What was she to do now? Antonia wondered angrily. Wait meekly here until he condescended to notice her again? Or go back to Perugia now without giving him that opportunity? No doubt there would be late buses on this *festa* night. If not, she could get a taxi. She made her decision without further delay and turned to push her way out of the square. She could ask someone where the buses could be found.

Then a voice exclaimed, "Antonia! Of all the surprises!"

Robert faced her.

"Hallo, Robert," she managed to mumble, then forced a smile.

"I'd no idea you were here," he continued. "Why didn't you let me know and we could have brought you with us? Cleo is here somewhere, but I seem to have mislaid her."

Antonia took a deep breath to prevent herself from blurting out where she had last seen Cleo "mislaid."

Robert linked her arm in his own. "D'you want to dance?"

It had been on the tip of her tongue to reply that she now had no heart for dancing, but she changed her mind and agreed. Why stand about like a wallflower waiting for a man who exhibited such bad manners as to leave her stranded in the middle of a crowd?

Even though Robert chatted lightheartedly as they danced, Antonia suspected that he was anxious about Cleo. He need not be, she thought bitterly, for .Cleo was at least being taken care of by Robert's friend and not a stranger.

For her part, she realised with some amazement that dancing with Robert was not at all the same as with Talbot, but gave her only a feeling of safety and comfort. Nothing intoxicating. Nothing magical. But she realised, too, that in the last few minutes her own feelings had changed.

"I must really look out for Cleo," murmured Robert. "If you catch sight of her, let me know."

Now was the time to tell him, Antonia knew, but she faltered. Talbot and Cleo might already have left the Piazza by now and be sitting in some secluded restaurant over a glass of wine.

"Did you come by bus today?" he asked after a few moments.

"No. I came with Talbot," she answered, steadying her voice.

His face became serious. "Oh, I see. But how did you become separated from him?"

She tried to smile. "We were torn apart in the crowd. I haven't seen him since, but no doubt he'll turn up in due course."

"I should hope so. He had no right to——"

"Leave me in the lurch?" she supplied his unspoken words.

"Well, it's a good thing I found you." But his mood had changed and she guessed that he was wondering if Talbot and Cleo were together.

The music stopped abruptly and the crowd thinned out, dispersing into side streets.

"Oh, there they are!" muttered Robert. Talbot and Cleo were drifting towards the corner of the Piazza and Robert and Antonia caught them up.

"Oh, Robert!" Talbot greeted him. "Glad we've all met up again."

I might as well not be here for all the notice he takes of me, thought Antonia angrily.

Cleo gave Antonia an angelic smile. "Have you been here all day? Robert was abominably busy," she continued without waiting for a reply. "We couldn't come until the afternoon."

The four now went to a small restaurant just the kind that Antonia had pictured where Cleo and Talbot might be enjoying each other's company without intrusive Robert or Antonia.

Cleo declared that she was starving and needed food, as well as wine. Robert flung out his hands in horror.

"No spaghetti, then, or your waistline will disappear, never to return," he commanded. His good spirits seemed to be recovered, but Antonia wondered if this was just a façade. Perhaps he was becoming really worried about Cleo's need for diversion, even when Robert was available.

Antonia was slightly disturbed by the almost severe glances she received from Talbot, but she was reassured by the thought that she would at least have the opportunity of driving home with him, whereas Robert and Cleo would be taking Robert's car. Then she would have the chance of asking Talbot why he had been so eager to abandon her in favour of Cleo. She would not put it as baldly as that, of course, but wrap it up in discreet words that would, however, leave him in no doubt as to how offended she was. She must be careful, though, or he would immediately taunt her with jealousy and making mischief.

But as it happened, such a journey was denied her, for Robert's car failed to start and he had to leave it for a garage to pick up. Cleo clapped her hands in an uninhibited gesture.

"You don't mind if I sit next to Talbot, do you?" she asked Antonia. "You've had him all day."

Antonia smiled and immediately slid into the back seat. Cleo's phrase made Talbot sound like a pet dog to be shared in turn. Well, perhaps that was all he deserved.

Robert sat with Antonia in the back and remained a glum companion while Cleo prattled gaily to Talbot, who spoke hardly at all except for an occasional "Yes" or "No."

It was a sad anti-climax to what had spelled, for Antonia at least, an almost perfect day of pleasure, a real festival occasion.

It was natural that he should drop Antonia first outside her *albergo*, since he and the other two all stayed at the Margharita. She did not know whether she would have welcomed a few minutes alone with him or whether it was better not to have the chance. She was too tired to argue, anyway.

"I'll send you your winnings," he called to her, as she alighted.

"Thank you. And thank you for a nice day's outing," she murmured.

"See you at the week-end at the site?" he asked.

"I'm not sure. I'll let you know."

In her room she flopped for a few minutes on her bed before she could summon up enough energy to undress, cream her face or brush her hair. She addressed a couple of pertinent questions to the slightly grimy ceiling. Why should I be so upset if he takes notice of Cleo? Am I allowing myself to expect too much of his attention when he told me so definitely that he had neither time nor inclination for girls?

The answers to these questions were not written on the ceiling and Antonia was too tired to dig out the truth for herself. Better not to bother about him. She had plenty to occupy her, especially now that she shared a studio.

Next day at the University for Foreigners in the Gallenga Palace she was almost too sleepy to think when the professor darted an accusing finger at her and told her to recount in Italian her day's outing at Gubbio. She faltered and he was patient, she stammered and he prompted, until at last she sat down in confusion, muttering that she would tell the story better another time.

"It is a pity not to share with us your exciting day," the professor sternly reprimanded her, while Ingrid and Sven and several of her other friends in the class smiled inquiringly at her and when lunchtime came, surrounded her, asking eager questions.

"Was your escort Italian or American?" asked the Swiss girl, as though there could only be two nationalities in the world.

Antonia shook her head. "Neither. English. He's the archaeologist for whom I've made some drawings at his excavation site. We really went to Gubbio partly to see the excavations there." Hardly true, but no matter.

"I wish we'd known about this Feast of the Candles," murmured Ingrid. "Sven and I and one or two others could have made up a party. Of course, we would not have crashed in on you and your Englishman." She gave an impish grimace. "In fact, we would have lost you and pretended not to see you, even face to face."

When Antonia arrived back at the *albergo* in the evening, a large parcel awaited her. Under the wrappings was not only a huge box of Perugina chocolates, but a note from Talbot.

"I hope you approve of my selection" he wrote, "instead of your own choice, but I believe in paying debts promptly. Best wishes. Talbot."

A wager discharged. Perhaps a friendship checked before it assumed demanding proportions, she thought. Well, it had not been her idea to beg him to take her to Gubbio for the Feast of the Candles. The suggestion had come from him, probably more for his own reasons of placating her so that her work at the excavations would not be interrupted by quarrels over Cleo.

She wrote him a note of thanks, not only for the chocolates but for the *festa* day. It was as brief and innocuous as she could word it, and she delivered it to the Hotel Margharita at the hall porter's desk.

As she reached the street again Talbot turned the corner sharply and almost cannoned into her.

"Sorry, Antonia, about that," he apologised.

"I left a note here to thank you for the chocolates, but you needn't have doubled the stakes."

"Why d'you try to throw all my kind-natured gestures in my face?" he demanded, but his tone was jaunty and his eyes amused.

"I didn't know that I was doing so. I didn't mean to."

"And another thing—oh, let's go into the hotel and have a drink or coffee or something," he suggested.

"I don't particularly want to stay long," she demurred. "I've a lot of my Italian homework to catch up."

"Can you spare me a quarter of an hour?" he asked with heavy sarcasm.

She smiled and allowed him to lead the way into the hotel courtyard.

When the drinks came, he leaned towards her. "Now, this bone I have to pick with you—why on earth did you abandon me like that last night in the square when we were dancing?"

Antonia nearly choked over her vermouth. "I? Abandon you? I thought I was the one that was tossed aside!"

He almost glared at her. "As soon as you caught sight of Cleo, you practically pushed me on to her and then you disappeared. I'd no idea where you'd gone."

"I met up with Robert, which was fortunate, but neither of us saw you or Cleo until after the dancing had ended."

He sighed. "I just don't understand the way girls' minds work. Before long I shall be in serious trouble with Robert if he thinks I'm trying to steal his girl."

"Am I to blame for that?" she demanded.

"Yes, I think you are."

"Oh, trust a man to find some way of pinning the blame on someone else whenever he knows or thinks he's in the wrong!"

To her surprise and annoyance Talbot began to laugh.

"What's so funny?" she wanted to know.

"You." He laughed again. "All right, let's just say that we were wrenched asunder by a wicked fate."

She finished her drink in silence and rose to leave.

"Of course," he said quietly. "Back to your Italian homework, but before you go, could I be allowed to ask timidly if you're coming to the site at the weekend?"

She gave him a straight, obstinate look, then smiled.

"I expect so, Saturday?"

He nodded. "Thank you. I'll pick you up at the usual time. Actually, something quite exciting has cropped up, not exactly on the site we've marked out, but near it."

Her interest immediately quickened. "A possible find?"

"It might be, but I'll tell you when we're there on Saturday."

He accompanied her through the courtyard to the street, and at that moment Cleo and her mother alighted from a taxi.

Antonia stayed only for the minimum of time to exchange brief greetings with the girl and her mother, then hurried along to the *albergo*. A smile crossed her face at the thought of Talbot's adroit dangling of the carrot before her, so that to satisfy her curiosity she would be committed to visiting the site when he expected her. If she had not met him outside the hotel tonight she would certainly have stayed away from the excavations and used her time for painting in her newly-acquired studio.

Talbot called on Saturday and took her to the site, where she worked until midday. So far there was no sign of Cleo, but that did not mean that the girl would not turn up if she chose.

Stefano joined Talbot and Antonia for the midday meal, since he had brought all the food and wine. Antonia longed to ask Talbot about the new discovery or possible finds, but thought it indiscreet to mention the subject in Stefano's presence. In the end, however, Talbot began to speak of it himself.

"We're trying to get permission to dig under Luciano

Pontelli's house. You've seen that young Italian boy who lives over there on the hillside."

"Yes, I remember him. He works to keep all his family and disapproved of me for grubbing about in the earth," replied Antonia.

"We don't know, but we think there may be a *hypogeum*, an Etruscan tomb chamber, more or less under the foundations of his house. It's really not much more than a shack."

"But it *is* Luciano's home and that of his family," she put in quickly.

Talbot waved away such an objection. "If he gives us permission, we could provide him with a much better one, a real house, either in the town or wherever else he wants it."

"What about the Government permit?" she asked. "Would you get that easily?"

"That is simple," Stefano said, "if one knows the right officials."

"D'you think Luciano will allow you to wreck his home?" she asked doubtfully.

"We're hoping he will if the reward is sufficiently high," asserted Talbot confidently.

"Do you know his terms yet?"

"We haven't progressed that far in the discussions," Talbot admitted. "At the moment it's a definite 'no,' but we hope to persuade him to agree."

In the evening after the day's work was finished, Talbot invited Antonia and Stefano to accompany him and drove his car as near as possible to Luciano's shack.

"I'd like you to meet his family," Talbot explained.

It was a poor enough dwelling in all conscience, thought Antonia, and surely a young Italian boy with the huge responsibility of providing for his family would jump at the chance of a new home and better accommodation.

The house built of random blocks of stone and pieces of wood seemed to cling to the slope of the hillside, but the inside was scrupulously clean with whitewashed walls, scrubbed tables and chairs and straw mats on the rough floor.

Stefano introduced Antonia to the Signora Pontelli, a small gaunt woman with a wrinkled face the colour of a dead brown leaf. There were two girls, Martina and Emilia, one perhaps eighteen, the other a couple of years younger. Both had beautiful dark eyes, faces with youthful curves and masses of almost black hair.

"Where is Luciano?" Stefano inquired.

"He is working," Antonia heard the mother reply.

She understood immediately why Talbot and Stefano had asked her to accompany them. In Luciano's absence, it would have been improper for two men to call when the boy's sisters were at home.

Even in so poor a house, there was a little wine to be offered and drunk with salutations. Antonia was full of compassion for this deprived family, but, more than that, her mind was busy with schemes to improve their conditions. First of all, she could try to provide the two girls, Martina and Emilia, with dresses, to replace the shrunk and faded cotton garments they now possessed.

As soon as she left the house with Talbot and Stefano and regained the car, she said to Talbot, "What do the girls do? Don't they work?"

"Luciano won't let them," replied Stefano.

"Why not? What's wrong?"

"He has the pride, you understand. He is head of the house and his sisters must be kept at home until they marry," Stefano explained.

"But that's Victorian!" she exclaimed. "It's positively feudal."

Stefano shrugged his incomprehension until Talbot explained the words to him.

"If Martina and Emilia worked at something, however humble," said Antonia, "they would earn a little at least for themselves and their clothes, and so help Luciano."

"Now you see why we're anxious to get him to agree to our digging," Talbot observed. "His sisters would

76

even have better chances of marrying reasonably well if only he'd take what we offer. They're not likely to meet men if they're cooped up in that hovel."

Stefano chuckled. "It is never wise to say that women are cooped up, my friend. Pretty girls always find a way out through the bars."

With his easy charm and flashing smiles, Antonia wondered if Stefano, on the pretext of business talks, had made an impression on one or other of the girls.

During the evening heavy showers of rain swept through Perugia, blotting out the surrounding valleys. When Antonia met her friends Ingrid and Sven at the Ricciotto restaurant for an evening meal, they were doleful about the weather prospects for the next day.

"We were going to swim at the Lido at Ponte San Giovanni tomorrow," said Ingrid. "They say the Tiber is nicer for swimming here than when it gets to Rome."

Sven shrugged his broad shoulders. "It does not look hopeful. The weather, I mean."

"Nor for me to go to the excavation site," agreed Antonia. "Look, if you don't go swimming, how about having dinner with me at the Margharita tomorrow night?" She was aware that she really owed them an occasional stylish meal in return for all the little bits of hospitality that Sven often paid for. "At least, if you can't swim, you could enjoy dinner in the evening."

Antonia promised to let them know by telephone next morning and confirm all arrangements. As she had expected, Talbot said that there was little point in going out to the site.

"Sometimes heavy rain brings us good luck, sometimes bad," he told her. "Depending on the slopes of the land, rain can wash half a week's work away for us, or it can uncover something we hadn't seen before. What are you doing today?"

"Painting," she answered with decision. "If I don't produce some pictures soon, my godfather will think he's merely given me money for a spree."

Francesca with whom she shared the studio had only

just risen when Antonia arrived about eleven. Several yawns and stretches later, she told Antonia that she was going out at about two o'clock for the rest of the day.

"So there is nothing to disturb you."

Antonia was glad that Francesca spoke little English, for it would be good practice, she thought, to speak so informally with a fellow artist. But, so far, Francesca had been too sleepy to talk much when Antonia was in the studio.

The Italian girl decorated pottery and made jewellery in addition to painting pictures, so she said. Possibly, thought Antonia, this earned her enough money at least to pay for canvases and colours.

Antonia had brought in enough food for a midday meal for both and offered some to Francesca, who made a wry grimace and declared she could never eat until evening, but she made coffee and the two girls chatted for a while until Francesca jumped up hastily and declared that she must dress.

Alone, Antonia took stock of her half-finished paintings and decided to work on a landscape showing a scene halfway down the valley between Perugia and Assisi. She tried to remember the expert Vittorio's injunctions about the quality of light.

She was so absorbed in her task that when she heard the studio door open, she subconsciously imagined it was Francesca returning for some purpose.

Only when a man said *"Buon giorno"* did she spin round to see Stefano standing there, smartly dressed, hat in hand and the happiest of smiles on his handsome face.

"Stefano!" she exclaimed in surprise. "How did you get in?"

"By the door, *signorina*, naturally," he replied.

"Not working at the site today, then?" She turned again towards her easel.

"Too wet. Besides, one does not work all the Sundays."

"How did you know I'd be here?" she asked a trifle crossly.

"But Francesca is my cousin," he replied blandly.

"Your cousin?" She swung round, palette poised in her left hand.

"She did not tell you this?" Stefano looked hurt.

"No, she did not. Not that it makes any difference. Well, Francesca is out today. She won't be back until late evening."

He shrugged. "No matter. Let me sit and watch you paint."

She was disconcerted, not because she objected to others watching her at work, for she had grown accustomed to that in art school. But Stefano's presence made her vaguely uneasy, although so far he had given her no cause whatever for disquiet.

She daubed at a few ineffectual strokes. Then she said, "I'll make you some coffee. Then I'm afraid you must leave, for I have a dinner engagement."

He nodded. "It is too early yet for dinner, so we can sit and talk, yes?"

There was nothing else to do but accept Stefano for a short time, then ask him to go.

She poured the coffee, handed a cup to Stefano, who was now lolling at ease in a dilapidated armchair by the window. She pulled up a stool and sat opposite him. At once he offered her the armchair, but she refused, for she knew it was far less comfortable than the padded stool.

There was a flirtatious look in his eyes, certainly, but perhaps he could hardly help that, and up till now he had behaved with complete propriety. In fact, she was wholly interested in his conversation, for he had told her a great deal about other archaeological digs he had worked on and the various objects found. Among other places, he had worked at Pompeii, where enormous excavations were going on all the time.

"You have been to Pompeii?" he asked.

"Not yet."

"Then you must stay a long time in Naples or Sorrento. Then you will be able to make many visits to Pompeii and see how they find whole streets and houses with gardens."

He leaned towards her to take her coffee cup. There was a slight tap at the door and Antonia unthinkingly called "Come in!" and then added, *"Avanti!"*

The door opened and Talbot stood there, his expression instantly changing from one of pleasurable greeting to a scowl.

"Oh, I see you already have company," he said brusquely. "I telephoned your *albergo* and was told you were here."

Stefano had already risen and now Antonia tried to maintain her composure.

"Did you want to see me particularly?" she queried.

"Not in the least. I thought we might have—dinner together." His words were clipped as though each separate one was punched out by a ticket machine.

"I'm sorry, Talbot," she said evenly. "I already have a dinner engagement."

"So I gather. Goodnight." He half closed the door behind him and Antonia and Stefano could hear his footsteps rattling down the wooden stairs.

"I'd better go now," said Stefano hastily.

"It would be as well," she answered gently. "Tell me more about Pompeii another time."

When he had gone, she stood in the middle of the studio, indignant, resentful, yet full of regret that Talbot had taken the trouble to visit the studio to invite her to dinner. Then again the insidious thought entered her head that Cleo was perhaps not available tonight and Talbot, tired of a wasted and wet day, needed a little diversion.

How dare he imagine that he could pick her up just when he had an idle hour or so? Then she laughed softly. If Stefano had been caught in the act of kissing and embracing her, Talbot could scarcely have shown more huffiness. As it was, she and the Italian had merely been chatting quietly over a cup of coffee.

Never had she been so glad that actually she would be dining tonight at the Margharita with her two friends, Ingrid and Sven. She hoped most fervently that they would be given a prominent table and that Talbot would not be able to avoid seeing them.

CHAPTER FIVE

ALTHOUGH Antonia was accorded her desire to flaunt herself and her two friends at a centre table in the Hotel Margharita's restaurant, there appeared to be no signs of Talbot. Towards the end of the meal, Robert approached the table, was introduced to Ingrid and Sven, and in the course of a few minutes' conversation disclosed that Cleo and her mother had gone to Assisi for the day.

Antonia was accordingly satisfied that Talbot had tried to avail himself of her company as a dinner companion, although why on earth he should take such trouble to seek her out, first at the *albergo*, then at the studio, she had no idea. Well, it would take him very little time to go down to Assisi by car and join the Norwoods, mother and daughter, if he knew where to find them. An amused flicker of thought sped across her mind. Would he have the courage to ask Robert which hotel or restaurant they might choose for dinner?

After dinner, Antonia and her two guests left the Margharita and went down to the Corso Vannucci to their favourite café in the Piazza Danti.

"Your English friend was not free tonight?" asked Ingrid, veiling her curiosity.

"He doesn't have to take me out to mid-week festivals, then saddle himself with me on Sundays as well," answered Antonia with a casual smile.

During the following week Antonia received several letters from home, including one from Philip Canford, her godfather, who wrote that he was thinking of spending several weeks in Italy, partly on business, the rest on pleasure, and hoped to stay in Perugia for at least a few days so that Antonia could show him the sights.

"Then I thought we might follow with a week or so in Florence," he had written. "It is many years since I was there and in those days I jammed every possible palace and museum and church into a few days, so that actually my recollections are now most vague. You and I could do things more leisurely now."

Once again Antonia was filled with gratitude that Philip had provided her with leisure as well as money to make the most of visiting these lovely cities.

On Friday evening after her classes had finished for the week, she sat on the steps opposite the graceful Fontana Maggiore, the Great Fountain, with its sculptured figures decorating the outside of the huge basin, and pigeons saucily washing themselves in the spray without a thought for the historical heritage on which they perched.

She had come to love Perugia for its contrasting character, its narrow medieval streets that seemed to hold memories of past enmities and treacherous vendettas. The violence and flaming passions between merchants and rival families, nobles and menacing intruders, had run their course, but the city, still girded with its old ramparts, dominated its hilltop, wrapping itself in a cloak of stone walls and glowering down the Umbrian plain.

Yet, even on this stormy evening when grey clouds scudded across the wide skies, it was possible to turn a corner and emerge without warning on to a belvedere, a small garden, the terrace in front of an hotel, and look down on the soft curves of the valley, a silvery stream flowing through olive groves.

When she returned later to the *albergo*, there was no message from Talbot and Antonia decided that she would not go to the excavations unless word came from him. She was not going to risk being snubbed for her pains.

She was about to go out for a meal when Robert telephoned.

"Have you plans for the week-end?" he asked.

"Why?" she asked cautiously.

"Talbot thinks it may be wet again and he doesn't want you to waste your time on the site. He has some other project on hand that he'd like to talk to you about. Could you come to the Margharita?"

"Now? Why can't he ask me himself?"

"He isn't here at the moment," replied Robert. "You can come and eat here just the same as going your own independent way down to the Piazza Danti."

After a few seconds' hesitation, she agreed. "All right. I'll be there soon."

She had not, however, bargained for dining with Cleo and her mother. So evidently Cleo was to have some part in the new project, too. Mrs. Norwood kept the conversation skilfully circling around harmless topics such as sightseeing, the various visits she and Cleo had made to Assisi, Orvieto and other places.

Antonia, in her turn, mentioned that her godfather, Philip, was soon coming to visit her in Perugia and possibly they would spend a few days in Florence.

Mrs. Norwood smiled. "Of course! I keep insisting that we really must go soon to Florence ourselves before the summer becomes too hot, but Cleo has become so interested in Perugia and its art and all the excavation discoveries that have been made in the past that she finds it hard to tear herself away."

Cleo smiled lazily, but her blue eyes remained hard as cut glass.

No mention, of course, thought Antonia, of the archaeologist who was perhaps Perguia's even greater attraction for Cleo.

When the meal finished, Antonia became slightly uneasy. Talbot had not yet put in an appearance. Should she seek out Robert and ask him where she could find Talbot? Was he waiting somewhere for her and getting angrier every minute at her non-arrival?

She was on the point of excusing herself to Mrs. Norwood when Talbot came into the courtyard.

He sat down for a few minutes, then spoke to Antonia. "If you're ready now, we'll go along to the store-room where I can show you what's to be done."

Cleo rose immediately. "Store-room? Oh, Robert mentioned that you had a kind of Bluebeard's chamber with all sorts of treasures in it. May I come, too?"

Antonia caught the look of resignation on Mrs. Norwood's face. Was she becoming disquieted by her daughter's eagerness for Talbot's society wherever opportunity offered or had she already accepted the fact that Cleo had swerved away from Robert?

The small store-room was in a basement. A long rough table laden with several trays of earth, broken pottery and tiles stood under the window grating.

"I'm providing you with a wet-weather job," Talbot said to Antonia. "It's a case of sorting out the pieces and fitting the jigsaws together. I have an expert who will then cement together any completed vases or urns and so on."

"Oh!" Cleo's face fell. It was evident that she had been expecting a much more glamorous job than this. Antonia had already discovered that archaeological "digs" consisted mostly of dust or mud, according to the weather, with occasional excitements when a "find" turned up.

"What's the weather forecast for tomorrow?" asked Antonia. "Dry enough for the site or wet enough for me to stay here?"

Talbot laughed. "Unpredictable, I think." Then Antonia thought she caught the whispered words "like women", but she was not going to be drawn into that kind of discussion, especially with Cleo prowling about the room examining the wooden cases which ostensibly contained further promising material.

When the three emerged on to the ground floor of the hotel, Mrs. Norwood was waiting with Robert, who had changed out of his formal dinner jacket into more casual clothes.

"Are you ready, Cleo?" called Mrs. Norwood, "Robert and I are waiting."

"Shan't be more than a minute," replied Cleo vanishing into the lift.

"Twenty minutes, she means," muttered Robert, while Mrs. Norwood smiled and shrugged amiably.

Antonia imagined that some evening amusement had been planned for the four, including Talbot, and since she did not want Mrs. Norwood to be obliged to invite her, Antonia prepared to leave the hotel.

She said goodnight to Mrs. Norwood and Robert and turned towards Talbot.

"I'll come outside with you, Antonia," he said. "I need some fresh air."

An odd remark, she thought, from one who had been out in the open most of the day. She accompanied him in silence and he led the way to the "balcony" in the Piazza that overlooked the plain towards Assisi. Here, if anywhere, one could breathe great gusts of fresh air.

"I didn't want to mention the matter in front of Cleo," he began after a moment or two. "She's such a prattle-box that she'll chat about it everywhere."

"Yes?" prompted Antonia, wondering what was coming.

"I've a suspicion that somewhere, either near here or outside Florence or even, perhaps, between here and Rome, there's a fake kiln. Etruscan vases are being manufactured. Jewellery, too. It's quite probable that they've secured some genuine articles, which rightly ought to have gone to the museums, and are now mixing the real with the fake."

Antonia's face became animated. "I'd no idea that crime extended to Etruscan pots. Is it easy to deceive the experts?"

"That depends on how well the fakes are made."

"What effect does it have on your work?" she asked.

"I mean, does it cheapen the value of anything you find?"

"It does, of course, to some extent. Fortunately, I'm more interested in discovering tombs and burial chambers that can't be removed, but only revealed. All the same, if we found anything really exciting like a unique piece of jewellery or a good bronze ornament, it would be maddening to find that its scarcity value had been cut down by imitations."

"Yes, I see that," Antonia agreed. "What are you going to do about it?"

"Nothing yet, but I wondered if you'd like to accompany me tomorrow to Lake Trasimeno. I expect you've already been there."

"No, I haven't," she replied. "I caught a glimpse of it on the way from Florence, but I've not yet visited it."

"There are two places I'd like to look at," he continued. "The town on the shore, Castiglione, is Etruscan in origin and I have a friend who has a villa nearby. He has a good collection of Etruscan and Roman stuff and he'll show it to us."

"Why d'you want me to come?" she queried.

"I could say I hate driving alone." He turned to smile at her. "You could come just for the ride. But more than that, I want you to make sketches, just rough ones, and I'm taking one of the cameras. Between us, we ought to get some results."

Antonia was slightly mystified as to what kind of results he expected, but she was more than willing to accompany him on a jaunt.

The owner of the villa by the lake shore was an Englishman married to a plump Italian wife with sparkling eyes and blue-black hair. The house was comfortably furnished with elegant taste, but there were so many antiquities scattered about that the atmosphere was that of an informal museum. Etruscan vases and fragments of tablets with inscriptions, small figurines or pieces of statuary were casually placed on tables or windowsills.

After lunch, Talbot began taking photographs of some of his host's collection. One piece particularly captivated Antonia's attention, a bronze chariot with horses and driver.

"If we could have it perched on this table," suggested Talbot, "and you, Antonia, could revolve it all quite slowly, I think we could get some interesting film."

As she carried out his instructions, she wondered if any photograph or cine-film could do justice to the intricate workmanship of that unknown artist who, two thousand five hundred years ago, had fashioned his galloping horses and spirited driver with such magnificent skill.

The gardens were an even greater revelation, for a vine-covered pergola was dotted with beautiful statues and ornamental seats. At one point a wall had been specially built to accommodate a collection of fragments of walls with inscriptions, each piece being set within a deep niche to protect it, presumably, from the effects of weather.

"Don't they deteriorate out in the open like this?" Antonia asked.

"That depends on the climate," replied Charles, the owner. "At home in England they'd become more grimy because of the damp air, but here they're less affected by wet. Long, dry summers help, too."

"How many fakes have you, Charles?" Talbot asked with a grin as the party strolled about the lawns that sloped down to the lake shore.

"None, I hope, although one can never be quite sure." He laughed. "The museum authorities will have to find that out for themselves when I'm dead. I intend to leave the villa as it stands, completely furnished, to the Perugian province."

Antonia had already wondered why he had been allowed to keep all these treasures instead of handing them to the museums, but now she understood.

She had brought her sketch-block with her, but so far Talbot had given her no instructions as to any drawings. Eventually, when Talbot had taken all the photographs he needed, Charles led the way down to a landing stage where a small motor dinghy was tied to a post.

Talbot and Antonia waved their goodbyes to Charles and his wife, and the boatman headed the dinghy for one of the three islands in the lake.

"He speaks only Italian," called Charles. "D'you think you can manage?"

"I have Antonia here to act as interpreter," Talbot shouted back.

Antonia grimaced. "That depends on how quickly someone speaks or what kind of accent he has. I'm not used to local dialects." She had assumed that the man in question was the one whom they were now on their way to visit.

On landing at the Maggiore island, Talbot instructed the boatman to wait for them. "We shall be at least an hour, perhaps more," Antonia heard him say.

A small medieval town with mellow stone or pink-washed houses prompted Antonia to say, "I must come here one day and paint these fascinating little corners and vistas."

"Why not wait until I take some successful photographs? Then you can copy those without the trouble of coming here and sitting in the hot streets with a small group of boys staring over your shoulder."

"What d'you take me for?" she said indignantly. "I suppose if I wanted photographs or coloured slides, I could find better ones than yours."

"I thought that remark of mine would needle you," he said with a complacent laugh. "You don't give me any credit for choosing excellent viewpoints, do you?"

"How would you know if your viewpoints pleased me as much as they suited you?"

He turned to glance at her. "All right. You choose."

"What use would that be when I haven't a notion of what particular piece of architecture or collection of buildings you're interested in?" she demanded.

"You have a certain logic," he conceded. He turned down a narrow street and led her through an arched doorway. "This is where we call on our friend."

The sudden transition from dazzling sunshine into the darkened gloom of the interior temporarily unsighted Antonia, but after a few moments, she was being introduced to Mario, an elderly man, thick-set, with a plump olive-skinned face and a bald head.

Antonia managed to follow the conversation between the two men and gathered that Mario had some very special exhibits. In a few minutes he had set out on a long table a collection of vases and jewellery.

"This is where you come in, Antonia," directed Talbot. "We'll tell you in a moment which ones we want you to sketch."

But her attention was absorbed by the beauty of the gold ornaments, brooches and pendants placed in front of her. She had never seen before such delicate engraving of pattern and design, and it was difficult to believe that these objects had lain in the earth in tombs for so many centuries and now shone with a satin sheen as though they had left the goldsmith's hands only the day before yesterday.

"Look for the Assyrian features," Talbot was saying to her. "This detailed head on the pendant, for example, and make it much larger in scale. We can enlarge the drawing still further when we get back."

He set up his camera at the same time and took several shots of a bronze urn with four spouts in the shape of camels' heads.

Antonia worked quickly but as accurately as she could, wondering why Talbot bothered with the human fallibility of sketching when he could have taken far more accurate photographs. No doubt he had a purpose in mind.

In a short time the two men left her alone in the room while they went down to a cellar to view other treasures.

As she sketched she noticed that each piece of jewellery, each vase was numbered, so she put the appropriate numbers on her drawings.

Talbot and Mario returned and both men studied the drawings she had already finished. Mario nodded his head with approval. Talbot gave no sign either way, but when Mario went away to fetch wine, Talbot muttered, "Yes, these might be useful because you don't know what you're actually copying."

"I thought it was Etruscan jewellery," she said.

"So it is."

"I see. Some of it may be fake?" she suggested.

He gave a warning "sh!" as Mario returned with the wine.

She and Talbot left the house about an hour later and returned to the boat which would take them across to the mainland.

At the villa, Charles asked "Successful?"

"I think so," replied Talbot.

"Sure you won't stay to dinner?"

"Thanks very much, but I'd rather get back. We'll have something on the way."

When he was driving along the lakeside road, Talbot said, "We'll have dinner at a little hotel in Tuoro. That's the small town whose claim to fame is that it's near the spot where Hannibal fought the Romans."

"And chased them into the lake, so I've read," she replied.

"History isn't the only reason why I wanted to be on the move and decline Charles's invitation to dine there. I've another call to make some distance from Tuoro."

When they arrived in the small pleasant town, Talbot warned Antonia not to leave her sketch-block or the drawings in the car. She noticed that he carried the camera with him into the hotel.

"Let's have fish," he suggested. "The lake is famous for roach, carp, eels, all kinds of fish."

At the end of the meal there were little cakes made with pine-seeds, which caused Antonia to laugh. "Never did I think I'd be sitting munching cakes like this. I've eaten beech-seeds in the woods, and when I was young and silly enough, acorns, but never before pine-seeds."

"Now you know that there are thousands of delicious edible things in the world."

When they returned to the car, Talbot said, "Give me the drawings you made at Isola Maggiore, but keep the sketch-block." He placed them in a folder, then on the back seat inside a newspaper.

He drove away from the lake in a northerly direction and stopped outside a house on the fringe of a village.

Inside, almost the same procedure was followed as at Mario's. The display of Etruscan jewellery, vases, urns, a stone effigy probably from a tomb, but although Talbot photographed almost the entire collection, Antonia was asked to make only two sketches, one of a bracelet, the other of a beautiful gold brooch with a long bar carved with a procession of animals.

This time the owner of the collection was a young man, Piero, with curly black hair and a flashing smile.

Part of the time he sat at Antonia's elbow and watched while she worked. When the visit was over, there were profuse thanks and prolonged farewells. Finally Antonia and Talbot were driving away along a road that would loop back to the main road to Perugia.

A sudden thought needled into Antonia's mind. "The sketches, Talbot. I gave them to you. Have you got them?"

He smiled gently. "No. I also gave the young man time to take the film out of the camera."

"But that means—that we've wasted our time!"

"Not quite. An hour, perhaps, with you sketching and my photographing, but we've learned that that young man, Piero, has a very good reason for not wanting his collection exposed to the examination of experts."

"Was it all fake?" she asked.

"I'm not expert enough myself to know that, but

I should guess about half and half. Some real, some fake."

"Then what can be done about it when we've lost all the evidence?"

"Not all. I took two of the drawings you made at Mario's into the house with me and swapped them for the two that Piero was so eager to retain."

"But you've still lost all your camera film."

He smiled quietly. "Yes, that's so, but it contains nothing except those pictures I took in his house. I don't want to alarm him too much or else he'll soon clear all the stuff out of the place. Two drawings accidentally left behind won't scare him so much, and of course he believes that we won't find out about the missing film until we arrive home."

Antonia digested this piece of reasoning. Then she said, "I'd no idea there was so much skulduggery in the archaeological antiques business."

"What goes on might surprise you. Now you see why I had to ask you to make drawings, some unnecessarily, in Mario's house, although naturally I didn't tell him the real reason."

After a long pause he said, "Don't mention the object of today's outing to anyone else, Antonia. Just a trip to Lake Trasimeno, a very usual week-end excursion."

"I shan't talk about it," she reassured him. "But thank you for bringing me. The weather was brilliant after all in spite of the stormy forecast."

"Sometimes it's the sudden storms that blow up when the forecast was fine that are more disconcerting," he answered, his attention fixed on the traffic as he emerged into the main road.

She smiled quietly to herself. She did not imagine that he was referring to the weather, but possibly to outbreaks of temperament among his associates.

"Have you made any progress with digging under the house where Luciano lives with his family?" she asked after a time.

"We hope so. He hasn't agreed anything yet, but we have to work on his family with gentle persuasion."

"It sounds like blackmail," she commented.

"Perhaps it is," he agreed, "but we need that site very badly. So far we haven't found much to justify the expense of digging over the area we've chosen. A few fragments of pottery, odds and ends of bronze."

"But you can't dig up the whole of central Italy to find just what's underneath."

"No. That's why I'm so anxious to explore from Luciano's place. D'you want to come to the site tomorrow if it's reasonably dry? Or are you painting in the studio?"

She hesitated before replying. "What I think you mean is—am I entertaining Stefano in the studio? Perhaps you'd better let me know first if you expect him to work on the site with you."

"No. I can't often use the men on Sunday's except in emergency. Why shouldn't you entertain Stefano if you want to?"

"I didn't particularly want to, but he came to the studio to see Francesca, with whom I share it. She's his cousin."

Talbot flung back his head and roared with laughter.

"What's funny?" she wanted to know.

"His cousin! Surely you're not so naive as to be taken in by that phony tale. Anywhere in Italy people go about claiming cousinship if it suits a purpose. Sometimes there is a remote relationship, but in ninety-nine cases there isn't."

"Well, I suppose Francesca could confirm it, I'll ask her," declared Antonia crossly.

"She'll immediately tell you that he is. Italian girls can't be expected to remember every single cousin, first, second or seventh, they possess."

Antonia smouldered in silence for the next few miles. Then the road curved to give a view of Perugia on its hilltop, a city wrapped in a dark cloak of night, spangled with a few flickering lights. .

"You still haven't told me what you want to do to-morrow," Talbot reminded her quietly as they drove up the zigzagging road to the city centre.

"If the men are not working what d'you intend to do?" she countered.

"You could help me with instrument readings."

She gave him a quick smile. "All right, I'll come." In spite of her occasional antagonistic feelings towards him, she was flattered that he seemed to want her help sometimes.

When she went to her room at the *albergo*, she remembered to sort out the dresses that she intended to take for Luciano's sisters. She would have preferred to buy new ones instead of giving away two or three of her own, but this would offend the family's pride and Luciano might be furious. In this way she could pretend that the dresses had shrunk and no longer fitted her or find other reasons for discarding them.

She was ready next morning at the usual time, but Talbot failed to call for her. She sat on her room balcony for an hour, then decided to go out to her usual café for breakfast.

When she returned there were apparently no messages or telephone calls, and she wondered what had gone wrong. She could at least telephone Robert at the Margharita.

"No, he isn't here, Antonia," Robert told her. "I don't know if he went to the site today."

"Would Cleo know that?" she asked. It was most unlikely, but Antonia had to frame her question obliquely, for she could hardly ask Robert point-blank if Talbot had taken Cleo out today.

"Hold on and I'll find out," he promised. After a long pause he came back on the line. "I'm afraid she went out quite early, her mother says. She thinks to Orvieto."

"Oh, I see," murmured Antonia. "Thank you, Robert."

"Come along here to lunch if you like," he invited.

"No, I must try to do some painting while I have

the chance or your friend Vittorio will tell me I'm lazy and idle."

"Then come in the evening. *After* dinner, if you want to be so independent."

"I'll see how I get on today," she told him, and replaced the receiver.

So today it was Cleo's turn for an excursion. But why the secrecy? Why on earth couldn't Talbot have told her straight that he was taking Cleo out? Perhaps there were also fake Etruscan pieces to be found in Orvieto and he had counselled Cleo to keep her mouth shut and on no account breathe a word to the "prattle-box, Antonia."

Yet, of course, she could not be sure that Cleo and Talbot had gone anywhere together.

She walked through the Sunday strollers to her studio where Francesca was at least half awake, if still drowsy.

"What on earth d'you do that makes you so tired in the mornings?" Antonia asked her.

Francesca yawned. "Go to bed too late, I expect. But that is when I feel most vital. Midnight. That is when I can talk and dance and feel that life is wonderful, if naturally I have a man to talk to and dance with." She yawned again.

"Let me make you some coffee," offered Antonia. "Then I shall start my painting, but you can sleep again if you want to."

"What is the weather like?" queried Francesca.

"Cloudy. Dull. No sunshine yet."

"Yesterday there was a bad storm. Thunder, lightning, rain like a waterfall."

"Oh?" Antonia was surprised. "I was out at Lake Trasimeno and it was fine there all day." A thought chased across her mind. If a storm had broken yesterday, was it possible that Talbot had gone out to the site much earlier than he had intended in order to inspect any damage?

"Your cousin Stefano came last week when you were out," she said later to Francesca.

"Stefano? Which Stefano?"

"I don't know his surname. He is a photographer and works with Mr. Drury on the excavation site."

Francesca shook her head. "I have so many cousins, here, in Florence, in Pisa; everywhere there are cousins. I cannot remember the one you speak of. If he comes again today I shall know which one he is."

Antonia thought it might be amusing if Stefano called and Francesca did not recognise him as one of her innumerable relatives, but of course things never turned out quite like that.

Stefano did not put in an appearance. Francesca stayed in until the evening although she did no work, but lounged about on a shabby old sofa padded with cushions.

"I work all the days in the week," she explained. "Sundays I like to rest so that in the evening I can be gay."

"And dance half the night so that you're fit for nothing on Monday mornings," Antonia spoke teasingly in English instead of the mixture of Italian interspersed with English that she had used so far.

"What is it you say?" Francesca raised one eyebrow.

"Oh, nothing. I was only teasing you."

Just before the light grew too dim for good work. Antonia asked Francesca, "What is your opinion of this picture?"

Francesca observed the painting for several minutes and Antonia waited.

"Some of it is good. The fields, the wall, the earth which is in shadow, but the sky—oh, no. It is not shining."

"You mean not luminous?"

Francesca nodded.

"I find it so hard to get it right," confessed Antonia.

"You must visit the museums and galleries. Regard our own Perugino and Pinturicchio. They have the light in their paintings."

Antonia sighed. "I think I shall never learn to paint Italian skies."

Francesca sprang up and began to dress and make-up ready for her evening date. Antonia smiled at the sudden energy that the Italian girl could display when the matter in hand was pointed towards pleasure.

As soon as she had cleaned her brushes and scraped her palette she returned to the *albergo* to change her dress, but decided to have a quick meal at a café round the corner. If she went to the Piazza Danti she might easily meet Ingrid and Sven or some of the other students in her Italian class, and then Robert would believe that she was deliberately delaying in making an appearance at his hotel.

In the Margharita's courtyard she chose an unobtrusive corner table, ordered coffee and asked the waiter to let Signor Roberto know that she was here, but not to disturb him if he was still busy with hotel guests

Robert came about half an hour later and sat down heavily opposite Antonia.

"Tired?" she asked sympathetically.

"Not particularly. I've become accustomed to being on my feet for about sixteen hours a day." He laughed quietly. "My father thinks I'm crazy, but I don't feel inclined to settle down yet at an executive's desk in an office full of potted plants and gimmicky decorations."

He ordered more coffee and cognacs for both of them.

"Cleo not back yet, I suppose?" she ventured.

He frowned. "No. Apparently she skipped out early this morning and didn't even tell her mother who were her companions. Oh, I know she's always been unpredictable, but there are times now when I could shake her in sheer exasperation until her teeth rattled out of her head."

"She's young," Antonia reminded him.

"I know that," he exclaimed, "but she could behave a little more normally, even for her age, and not give us all this worry."

"Robert, perhaps it's the same kind of feeling that you have. You've just told me that you don't want to be tied down to your father's business yet. Cleo probably doesn't want to be tied down to one man yet. You must try not to let her think that you want her on the end of a chain or she'll break away. Be patient."

"I wish I could." His eyes were sombre. "I love her very much. I want to make her happy because it's the only way I'll ever find happiness myself."

At this moment Antonia believed that she saw with remarkable clarity that the time would never come when Robert found his happiness with Cleo, unless it were ten years hence when the girl who had received everything and been denied nothing had been tempered through the fires of passion and the waters of grief. Cleo was too mercurial to be wholly attracted by a good match with a wealthy man's son, even though on his side Robert genuinely adored her.

How long would it be before Cleo tired of the novelty of attention from an archaeologist?

"I wish I could help you," Antonia murmured.

He raised his head and squared his shoulders. "Oh, well, I suppose I must wait until she grows up a bit. By the way, Talbot's down in the store-room if you want to see him for any reason."

"Talbot? Didn't—didn't he go out with Cleo then today?"

"Good heavens, no! He went off at crack of dawn to the site. There was heavy rain there yesterday and he went out to see if damage had been done. Or even if it might have helped by uncovering objects. It does, sometimes."

Antonia rose. "Didn't you know this when I telephoned you this morning?"

"No. I wasn't on duty then. I found out later." Then his face clouded. "I wonder if Cleo really went to Orvieto or Talbot to the site."

Antonia felt a sudden twinge of compassion. She had put unworthy suspicions into his mind. Why did she have to mention Cleo?

"I'll go and see Talbot," she muttered. "Thanks for the coffee and brandy, Robert. I'll see you later, perhaps."

She hurried away in the direction of the store-room, knocked on the door and entered. Talbot had apparently just finished dinner off a tray. His clothes were streaked with mud, his face and hair grimed, but his features held a triumphant expression.

"Hallo, Antonia! I think we're on to something at last. As soon as I heard about yesterday's storm I went out as soon as possible."

"I thought you wanted me to take readings of some instruments or other," she said coolly.

"There was no question of that. I—" he stopped. "Oh, yes, I expect I ought to apologise for not calling for you. Don't tell me you had a wasted day."

"Of course not. I painted half a masterpiece, the kind that lies only in the eyes of its painter."

"I'm sorry I couldn't wait. I grabbed Stefano out of bed and took him with me. Two trenches have caved in, full of water at the bottom, but the rain scoured part of the hillside and brought down great lumps of earth and boulders. I've left some of those to be dried off in the kiln and I'm hoping we might have something of interest when we bake off the clay. I'm convinced more than ever now that Luciano's house is close to the entrance to a tomb."

"I know it's necessary," Antonia said, "but it sounds so macabre always to be talking of exploring tombs."

He turned to face her. "But, Antonia, you know perfectly well that Etruscan tombs are practically the only monuments available that will give us any idea at all of what the people were like and how they lived. Their tombs became miniature examples of their palaces, or, at least, the interiors; they had effigies made of themselves and placed them on top of the sarcophagi. They made sculptures and paintings of scenes of their lives, their sports, like wrestling and hunting. We wouldn't even know how they made music if we hadn't found representations of pipes and flutes, which the Romans subsequently copied."

He stopped and took a deep breath. "Sorry to be carried away like that, but I forget sometimes that my kind of life work isn't necessarily everyone else's."

She smiled at him. "I don't mind. I like to hear you talk so eloquently about the past."

"Sit down here with me and help me sort out these odds and ends," he invited. He carefully unpacked a wooden box of what appeared to be nothing but rubble and showed her how to lay out even unlikely-looking fragments on a flat diagram so that the shape of a rounded bowl or vase might possibly fall into place.

"I see," she said with some enthusiasm. "It's like a paper pattern of a hat, for instance. When you curve the edges together, it makes a crown."

He gave her an oblique glance and his eyes gleamed. "You have a genius, Antonia, for reducing my high-level art and archaeology to the homeliest of everyday terms."

"But that's what you wanted. The home life of the Etruscans exactly as they went about their daily chores."

"I wish we could find more of it," he sighed.

As they sorted and tried to fit the jigsaw pieces, he told her of some of his other projects.

"In Syria we found this inscription on a stone wall and of course we made a plastic facsimile and sent it home to the British Museum to be deciphered. Eventually we heard how delighted they were to receive it because this was one that many years ago someone else had discovered and sent them a facsimile in *papier-mâché*. By the time the experts started to decipher, they found that mice had taken a great liking to the *papier-mâché* and eaten away a good many lumps. A good invention, plastics. At least they're inedible to mice."

"What scholarly mice!" exclaimed Antonia, laughing. "But you'd think a museum's own tribe would at least wait until the inscription was deciphered before making a meal of it."

She tilted back her head and laughed again, then broke off as the door was violently flung open and Cleo stood there, her face flushed with anger and surprise.

"How cosy!" she cried. "So this is why you couldn't join us to go to Orvieto today. We waited ages for you, but you didn't turn up. Obviously, you had better ways of spending the day."

Antonia sat calmly, but Talbot rose and glared at her.

"I told you last night, Cleo, that I wouldn't be coming. If it interests you, I've spent all day at the site, wading about in mud."

"With Antonia to keep you company?" Cleo demanded.

"No," snapped Antonia. She rose now. "I'll go now, Cleo, and leave you and Talbot to sort out your tangled arrangements. Goodnight."

In the hotel hall she met Robert, who gave her an anxious look of inquiry.

"I expect you know that Cleo has returned," she said in a low, but stormy voice. "What on earth has made her so excited?"

To her complete surprise, Robert smiled and clasped his hands in one resounding clap. "Good! It's worked."

"What has? What are you up to?"

"I told her that Talbot was down in the store-room waiting for her."

"But not that I was also there?" she asked.

He nodded. "Antonia, I've got to do something to break up this—er—this imagined crush that she has on Talbot. You know perfectly well that he isn't the marrying kind, or at least, not until he's about fifty and wants a wife to play hostess to his professor friends. Cleo doesn't realise that."

"And she never will if you play this kind of trick on her," retorted Antonia. "Why don't you have the sense to leave her alone for a while? If you're ever going to be happy together she'll soon come back to you. But for heaven's sake, give her a chance for a fling. And next time you want to rouse her to jealousy, don't involve me."

Robert sighed. "I thought you'd understand."

"Perhaps I do understand Cleo better than you do. Stirring her up to stupid scenes like that just makes her more wilful and determined to show you that she can easily get six other men on a string." After a pause, she added, "You'd better go down to the store-room now and see if Cleo is crying and being comforted in Talbot's arms. If she is, then you've only yourself to blame."

She walked quickly out of the hotel towards the *albergo* where she lived. The last quarter of an hour had been charged with stormy, if rather childish, emotions, but it was Robert's words that pierced her mind and repeated themselves over and over. " . . . not the marrying kind . . . not until he's fifty . . . a wife to play hostess . . ."

Oh, yes, Antonia knew all that. Talbot Drury had made no secret of his lack of interest in women and the way in which he intended to run his life. So it might be prudent for her as well as Cleo, to understand and remember his attitude. Not that there was any need on her part. For all his handsome fairness of looks and athletic strength of body, he was not the sort of man with whom Antonia would ever fall in love.

CHAPTER SIX

DURING the week Antonia received news from Phillip, her godfather, that he would arrive in Perugia within the next ten days and would let her know the exact date as soon as he could.

She sighed with relief at the prospect of spending a little time in his company, then perhaps visiting Florence and Pisa without the webs of cross-currents caused by Robert and Talbot with Cleo as the apex of their triangle. Let them sort out their problems while she and Philip strolled by the banks of the Arno and pottered on the Ponte Vecchio.

Towards the end of the week she telephoned Talbot, whom she had not seen since that incident last Sunday in the store-room.

"So if you want me to come to the site any part of this coming week-end," she explained, "I shall be available. After that, I might be in Florence or somewhere else with Phillip."

"Yes, I see. Come Saturday and this time I promise to pick you up without fail."

It occurred to her that she might spend the evening after dinner in the store-room working on piecing the fragments together. No doubt Talbot would not want to keep his expert cement-worker waiting with nothing to do.

At the Margharita she asked Robert for the store-room key.

"Is anybody working down there now?" she asked with a smile.

He laughed in return. "Not this time."

She had not been working at the trays and diagrams for more than half an hour when Cleo came quietly into the room.

Antonia politely greeted her and shifted her place farther up the table to make room for Cleo to sit down.

"I'm not staying more than a minute or two," Cleo told her. "I came to apologise to you for my outburst the other night."

Antonia was surprised, but hoped that her face did not betray her.

"Oh, it's all right." She made a vague, dismissive gesture. "You'd probably had a tiring day."

Cleo remained standing, probably because she did not want to soil her white lace dress by sitting on grubby chairs or packing cases.

"It was very wrong of me to make a scene like that," Cleo continued, apparently determined on self-abasement, "but I think you must at least understand the position between us."

"Between *us*?" echoed Antonia, not yet diverting her attention from her task on the table. "There can't really be any position between you and me. I'm just a struggling artist lucky enough to be given the means of a year's foreign travel. You are the daughter of probably well-to-do parents and you're going to marry Robert—in due course."

"That's it. You're quite wrong," declared Cleo with a gentle smile. "I'm not going to marry Robert."

Antonia's head jerked up. "No? Have you changed your mind?"

"It was never my intention to marry him. Oh, I like him. He has great charm. More than that, he's honest, which I'm not." She chuckled at her confession.

"Then why did you let him think that you'd marry him?"

Cleo shrugged. "He was so pressing, so devoted, and it's always so useful where other men are concerned to be able to put up such a lovely fragile barrier with the words 'Touch me not. I'm promised to another.' " She met Antonia's stare of disbelief. "You see, I told you I wasn't honest."

Antonia turned her face away and remained silent.

"Don't you want to know what my programme is?" asked Cleo.

"Not particularly. Whatever you have in mind may only be a passing fancy."

Cleo laughed. "Oh, Talbot would love that description of himself. A passing fancy! I'm going to marry him."

Antonia would not allow herself to look at the other girl.

"Are you prepared to live his kind of life?" she asked.

"Oh, you mean all this archaeology stuff, digging up urns and tombs and things. Of course not! Use your imagination, Antonia dear. Can you see me messing about in trenches or deserts for the rest of my life?"

"I confess I can't," returned Antonia.

"Talbot will finish the work he's undertaken to do,

of course, here in Italy. It wouldn't be right to leave it half done. After that, we shall travel around for a while, then he'll be able to pick any kind of regular job he wants."

"Nine-to-five in a museum, I suppose!" Antonia swung round on her visitor. "Haven't you yet got it into your silly little head that Talbot's entire life is going to be spent in excavations of one sort or another? D'you think he'll ever be content to travel up to town everyday, read about other men's exciting finds and then travel home to a daintily-dressed wife, cocktails and after-dinner bridge?"

"You do feel strongly about the man, don't you?" Cleo's voice was a slow, contented drawl. "I'd no idea. But it won't do you any good. Once, you taunted me—when I first came to the digging site—about playing Cleopatra to his Antony, I wondered then if you really meant that you'd prefer to play Antonia to his Antony, I'm quite sure now." She pulled her silver stole around her shoulders. "I must go now. Talbot is waiting for me. Goodnight, Antonia."

After the other girl had gone, Antonia stared in front of her for a long time, not seeing the pieces of an almost completed vase laid out on a diagram, but visualising Cleo and Talbot together, not here in Perugia, but at home in England. How could Talbot allow such a girl to wreck his life, his ambitions, and surround him with the empty, smart-set silliness for which Cleo would crave?

Eventually Antonia decided that she could do no more work tonight. She locked the store-room and handed the key to the hall-porter. Then she hurried out of the hotel as quickly as possible in case Robert might be about.

But for the fact that Philip was due here in a few days' time, she would have gone straight back to the *albergo*, packed all her possessions, settled her accounts and taken the first train she could catch to Rome or Naples. Anywhere that would put her at a distance from Talbot and his idiocies. She was sorry now that she had provisionally booked a room for Philip at the Margharita instead of the Brufani Palace. It would only mean further meals in the company of Talbot, the Norwoods and Robert. She could, however, persuade Philip to go to Florence as soon as possible.

On Saturday morning as she drove with Talbot in the car towards the site, she made a great effort to appear normal. She chatted about Philip, about their plans for Florence, about her near-success with parts of a vase. Then he said:

"What's the matter with you? You're as talkative as a sparrow."

"If I were unduly silent you'd accuse me of sulking over something," she replied.

"You've gone to the other extreme, so now I know you're displeased over something. Spill it."

She smiled. How could she say to him that it worried her that he was about to make a fool of himself over Cleo? Or that she disapproved of his ethics in taking Cleo away from Robert?

"Oh, it was nothing," she said at last. "I get depressed over my painting and now that Philip is coming, I wanted to show him that his money had been reasonably well spent."

"Instead of which you frittered your time away on an excavation site, not to say day after day at the language University."

"Learning Italian could hardly be wasted," she reminded him.

"But excavations are a foolish pastime," he retorted quickly. "All right, that puts me in my place. I ought to have known after you called my work 'will o' the wisp' stuff."

"I certainly didn't. I was then considering whether it was 'will o' the wisp' stuff for me, not you."

By now they had arrived near Luciano's house and there was no opportunity for further argument.

Antonia had remembered to bring the small parcel of dresses for the boy's sisters.

Luciano was, of course, out working and she was glad of his absence, for he might have tried to prevent his sisters accepting any form of charity.

Martina and Emilia were delighted with a dress apiece and dashed off to another room where they could try on their new acquisitions. When they reappeared, Antonia noticed that Martina, the elder, had removed the scarf wound round her head, but her hair was cut short.

"I'm sorry I've had my hair cut off," she lamented. Then an appealing expression came into her eyes. "Do not tell Luciano. He will be very angry."

Antonia smiled and answered in her improving Italian, "Why should he? Your hair will grow again."

"It was the money, you understand," put in the mother. "One can sell to the hairdresser."

Antonia nodded. Of course! She had read many times that the best hair for wig-making and hairpieces came from the girls of central Italy. Poor Martina! So pinched for money that she had been forced to sell her beautiful hair.

The two girls paraded in their new dresses and Antonia, while complimenting them, made a mental note that they required sandals. Somehow she must contrive to know the right sizes. Most of their time they went barefoot, but they needed sandals for some occasions.

Talbot promised that he would call again on Luciano in the early evening and he and Antonia left to drive along to the main site where Stefano and his small gang of workmen were already scraping and brushing, poking delicately at corners with their pointed flat trowels or thin-bladed knives.

Today another man awaited Talbot, an Italian who turned out to be Signor Lombardo, an official from the Perugia archaeological museum. There was a long conference while Antonia sat on a camp stool and waited for instructions.

Eventually Talbot called to her, "Come along, Antonia. We're ready now." The trio walked back to the hillside above Luciano's house and two other men brought tripods and small folding stools. Talbot himself carried a curious instrument which she knew was a magnetometer, but she had only a hazy idea of its purpose.

Now she was told to mark her sketch-block into squares corresponding to the large chart which the museum director showed her.

"As I call out the readings, take them down against the number," instructed Talbot. "They won't be in the right order, but that doesn't matter."

The two men set up the magnetometer on its tripod a few yards away from the roof of Luciano's house. corroborated the readings in both languages, then Talbot called them out in English.

Together Talbot and the Italian moved the instruments from one position to another, shortening or lengthening the tripod legs according to the slope of the hill.

The man's excitement mounted rapidly and Antonia had never seen Talbot so exultant.

"It might turn out to be larger or better than the Volumni," she heard him say to his companion, whose face spread with delighted smiles.

The Italian made notes at great length, then Talbot came to Antonia, looked at her figures on the various sheets of her pad. He took her pencil and drew a ring around an area that took in several squares, spoke to the Italian, who apparently agreed.

"This is it, Antonia," Talbot said quietly, "but not too many words to anyone else. We think we've found a tomb of great importance. If we can get Luciano's permission to tunnel through from his house, it will save us an immense amount of work. If not, we'll have to start down from the top in a vertical line. I hope that won't be necessary. Signor Lombardo will help us with permits and so on now that he knows there is something here. It may, of course, turn out to be only a wall or a buried pottery kiln, but the instruments show something."

"What's the next move?" she asked.

"Luciano. Persuasion first."

"And if persuasion fails? What then?"

Talbot looked out into the hazy distance, the gentle contour of hills, the plains threaded with small streams on their way to join the Tiber. When he did not immediately answer she queried, "Force?"

"Either way I'm afraid his shabby little house will have to be destroyed. If we use it, then it's possible the foundations will collapse. If we strike down from the top, above his house, the same thing may happen. In any case, if there's really a tomb there, we shall need to build a good entrance for public access."

"How ruthless you are, Talbot," she said, with compassion for Luciano and his family.

"Heavens, girl, we're not out to destroy a noble work of art, a *palazzo*, a church of ancient origin. What we really have to thank Luciano's family for is that their little shack of a place has providentially masked our exciting discovery, although even now we don't know whether previous explorers have already ransacked that place and removed the treasures. It's just as likely that bands of robbers at one time or another have helped themselves to whatever they could find."

She smiled at him. "Whatever is there, I hope you're successful," she said. "But treat Luciano well. He deserves it."

After midday lunch in the tented "Agincourt" and the subsequent siesta, Signor Lombardo drove back to Perugia, promising to push through all necessary permits and documents as fast as possible.

"How will you be able to keep the possible discovery a secret from all the workmen here?" Antonia asked Talbot when no one else was about.

"It's to their interest not to blab. They get a basic rate of pay with a bonus for every likely interesting object they find. That's why the whole gang stops work when one member thinks he's on to something, so that it can be checked by Stefano or me and he can be credited individually for his results."

"I see."

"We'll go back to Luciano's about seven o'clock and see if he's home," suggested Talbot.

"What does he do for a living for all that family to keep?"

"He works all day in the fields for a vineyard owner. In the summer evenings he attends to his own crops, his onion rows and broccoli patch. All the winter he worked at nights as a washing-up boy in an hotel at Ponte San Giovanni, then walked home to get up at five or so to start his next day's work."

"But if he would only let his sisters earn a little money by working! They're not lazy girls, I'm sure."

"I believe Martina, the eldest girl, started as a daily maid in a house at a nearby village, but when Luciano found out, he brought her back home."

"Almost dragging her by the hair, I suppose, caveman style? Perhaps that's another reason why she's had her hair cut short."

When they arrived at Luciano's the household was in a considerable turmoil. The two girls, Martina and Emilia, were in tears and Antonia noticed they were wearing their oldest, most ragged dresses. The mother sat at the table, her head bowed, while the two younger children, a small boy and a girl slightly older, banged saucepan lids and spoons together, shouting at each other. Only Luciano remained calm in the midst of this din and confusion. He stood tall and straight, his head high, and handed Antonia a parcel, the same which she had brought containing the two dresses.

He bowed politely to Antonia, then to Talbot. "I am very sorry, *signorina*, but I cannot allow my sisters to accept gifts. We do not wish for charity."

"It isn't charity," began Antonia, but was interrupted by a wild outburst from Martina, who sprang up and tore the scarf from her head with a dramatic gesture.

"I will pay for the dresses with the money from my hair!" she exclaimed.

Luciano stared at her, appalled, his eyes blazing.

"You have sold your hair?"

Martina covered her face with her hands and turned away in a paroxysm of sobbing. "I wanted some money —to buy nice clothes—to look nice for—for—"

Antonia immediately guessed the reason for Martina's sacrifice. There was a young man near for whom the girl wanted to appear at her best.

"Luciano!" Antonia spoke quickly. "I apologise for giving your sisters the dresses. Please do not be offended, but I will certainly accept a little money for them. Then it's no longer charity."

Martina and Emilia turned frightened glances of inquiry towards Antonia, who gave a slight nod of reassurance, hoping that they would understand that this was a gesture to restore Luciano's pride and that the money would be returned secretly to Martina.

She named two small sums of lire and Luciano nodded, ordered Martina to pay the amount to Antonia, who carefully put the crumpled notes into her handbag.

Talbot, who had been standing just inside the doorway with his back to the family while this scene had taken place, now turned. "If your transaction is completed to everyone's satisfaction, Antonia, perhaps we could get along to the real business with Luciano."

Antonia was conscious of his sarcasm, but was it her fault that the boy had created such a scene over a couple of half-worn-out dresses?

"We will go outside the house," Luciano decided, and led the way.

Antonia tried to linger so that she could return the money, but Talbot obtusely came behind her and gave her no chance.

"I hope all this affair hasn't put Luciano into a more resentful frame of mind so that he's going to prove even more obstructive than he has been already," he said quietly to Antonia as they followed the Italian boy.

"Was it so thoughtless of me not to remember his abominable pride?"

Talbot sighed. "Your gifts might have been better timed. He suspects bribery in every direction. After the negotiations were settled would have been better to give the girls presents. He's a fierce little Perugian."

"I can well believe that. Four hundred years ago, he'd have gone out with a sword and run it through anyone who came in his way!"

Luciano had stopped and now indicated a rough wooden seat at the lower end of what might be termed his hillside allotment of cultivation.

"Here we shall be away from the noise of women," he remarked, but studiously averted his eyes from Antonia, who was, however, well aware that she was regarded as an intruder.

Talbot launched into a brief account of the recent experiments and added that a museum director had been here today and would undoubtedly secure the necessary permits for digging.

"My house is my home," declared Luciano with all the rebellious mutiny that a young boy could command. "Also for my family."

Once again Talbot put forward his arguments of how much better off in every way all the family would be in a better house. "Your mother would have comfort, your sisters have good dowries, you wouldn't need to work twenty hours a day. More than that, if there is something interesting under your house, then it would be open to the public, and perhaps the museum would put up a small plaque saying that this is where Luciano Pontelli once lived."

The boy remained silent and thoughtful for a while.

"Supposing I should tell other people that there is much gold here and they offer me more money than you?" he queried at last.

"Oh, you couldn't do that, Luciano!" exclaimed Antonia. "We were here first."

Talbot gave her an amused look which she translated as one of sardonic surprise that she should ally herself with him in that "we."

"So you'd accept an offer from the highest bidder?" asked Talbot of Luciano.

He shrugged. "Perhaps. Perhaps not any offers at all."

"If you had the money from us or anyone else," put in Antonia, "What would you do with it? What would you buy?"

"Many things."

"Such as?" she prompted.

"I don't know."

But she remembered that one day she had seen the boy with Stefano, who was explaining one of the cameras to him. If Luciano's Achilles heel should turn out to be a camera? Still, it was no use thinking of trying to bribe him that way. A couple of dresses for the sisters had proved troublesome enough already.

Talbot was speaking again. "You understand, Luciano, that if you do not agree to let us dig, when we get the permits, then you will still have to leave and we shall pull down the house. Naturally, you will get other accommodation, but you could also have the compensation as well."

He rose, indicating that he had said his final word. Antonia looked at the boy's face, vulnerable, young, puzzled by the ways of authority who would not leave him in peace to fend as best he could. Yet his obstinate pride governed his actions, even at the expense of his family.

She followed Talbot towards the house where a more peaceable atmosphere now prevailed. The mother was preparing the evening meal while Emilia played with the two smaller children. Martina was not there, so Antonia opened her handbag and quickly thrust the notes into Signora Pontelli's apron pocket.

The faces of mother and daughter were now alight with smiles of thanks as Antonia and Talbot said their goodbyes.

Along the path to Talbot's car, Antonia saw the reason for Martina's absence. In the shadow of a gnarled olive tree and out of sight of her home, the girl was laughing and talking with a young man, who took her hand, pulled her towards him and ruffled her short, thick hair. So evidently no lasting harm had been done as far as the young man was concerned.

"I hope he means well," muttered Talbot. "He's one of my workmen."

"I didn't know you'd even noticed the couple," she observed with a mischievous smile.

"Martina's light dress doesn't exactly blend in camouflage with the surroundings. If he's not very sincere and thinks Luciano's sisters are handy for anyone with a roving eye, there'll be the devil to pay."

Antonia hoped, too, that Martina was not taking the first chance of easy escape from the constrictive home life that Luciano imposed on the girls.

In the car, Talbot suggested that they might have dinner at a wayside inn, instead of returning immediately to Perugia.

She looked dubiously at her dusty jeans and not very clean shirt, then at his equally earth-stained clothes.

"Are we respectable enough?" she queried.

"I shall be when I've washed my hands and combed my hair," he answered smugly. "The inn that I have in mind will provide us with such simple facilities."

"What's good enough for you will certainly satisfy me," she retorted.

"I doubt it! Are you putting yourself on my primitive level? I thought you cared more for social status."

"What gave you that idea?" she asked. "Artists can't usually afford conformity, not until they're highly successful anyway."

"And then they can be eccentric." He turned to give her a quick glance. "I wonder how bearable you'd be as a successful artist."

She broke into laughter. "You don't need to worry about that remote possibility. Even Francesca, the girl who shares the studio, can see the most glaring faults in my work."

"Jealousy!" he declared.

In a few moments they had arrived at the inn, where they were given a table on the first floor roof garden.

"The food is simple here," Talbot remarked, "but you'll enjoy it."

The events of the day had driven from Antonia's mind all thoughts of Cleo and that unnerving scene last night and as she sat with Talbot over their coffee and liqueurs, she was content to enjoy his company while she had the chance.

"I wonder what Cleo is up to," he murmured suddenly, and Antonia's serenity was roughly torn apart. So even sitting here in the deepening twilight his thoughts were centred on Cleo. Yet why then had he suggested dining here and not returning very early to Perugia? Clearly he had apparently not bound himself to any particular arrangement that included Cleo.

"Out somewhere with her mother—or even Robert," answered Antonia, feeling that an occasional reminder that Robert existed might grate upon Talbot's sense of fair play if not his conscience.

"Not with either, I should think," he said. "That's what I mean. She seems to be playing some sort of game in which Robert is certainly going to be the loser if he's not careful."

Antonia stared at Talbot's face. Was he dissembling or was he really so innocent and ingenuous that he did not know every move of Cleo's game?

"Robert loves her very much," Antonia said quietly.

"I know. That's what makes the position so damnable." He spoke almost violently.

"In what way?"

"If she chucks him for someone else, Robert will take a long time to recover."

"What makes you think that she's going to chuck Robert?" she queried.

He shrugged. "Perhaps I'm wrong about it. Maybe it's the way all girls behave, thinking it's fun to stir up jealousies just to complicate matters."

"Is that your opinion of me?" she asked. "What jealousies have I stirred up?"

It was his turn now to stare at her in disbelief. "Tonia!" For the first time he had called her by her diminutive name. "You're not pretending surely that your entirely harmless friendship with Robert hasn't sometimes been designed to needle Cleo?"

"I'd never thought of it that way," she answered coldly. "Robert has been a most helpful friend to me ever since I came, but no more than that. I can't help what construction Cleo tries to put on a sincere and uncomplicated relationship, but I've never set out to make a conquest of him. I should have a low opinion of myself if I had done so. I leave it to Cleo to make the easy conquests."

A half-smile curved his mouth. "I really believe that Cleo gets under your skin," he said softly, in his most provocative tone.

She wanted to say, "And under your skin, too?" But she controlled herself sufficiently to murmur calmly, "Not in the least."

"I find her an exceedingly charming young thing," Talbot said.

"You should tell her so—often. She likes to be praised."

Talbot began to laugh. "I can see that it doesn't do to compliment Cleo when you're around. I should never have thought you were so envious of another girl's attractions. After all, you're quite pretty yourself."

"Thank you," she snapped. "What you really mean is that I'm not bad-looking, but I have no charm, no magnetism."

He sighed deeply. "No need to throw my poor compliments back in my face. Whatever I say now will be wrong."

Antonia remained silent, feeling that she had allowed herself to receive the worst of the argument. She had let him provoke her to rash retorts that betrayed her lack of sympathy with Cleo.

They left the inn soon afterwards, but neither spoke much on the journey home. As he drove down her street in Perugia, he asked. "What are you doing tomorrow?"

116

"Painting," she replied immediately. She knew better than to hesitate so that he could offer to take her out for an excursion because Cleo was otherwise engaged. "I told you that I must get some work ready to show Philip when he arrives so that he doesn't believe that I've wasted my time."

"Pity," he murmured. "I thought of swimming in the Lido at Ponte San Giovanni, and then I could also show you the Volumni tomb."

She gave him a bright smile. "Take Cleo instead. She'll love to have you for a guide."

Without giving him time to answer, she slammed the car door, crossed the narrow strip of pavement and hurried into the *albergo*.

She had been in her room some ten minutes or so when she chanced to step out on the balcony. Talbot's car was still in the street below, but as she watched he drove off down the street as though her unseen appearance had been a signal.

She flung herself into the rickety wicker-work armchair and reflected that she had handled the end of the evening very badly indeed. She had given Talbot the impression that she was mean and spiteful. Then she became suddenly surprised by the discovery that this was probably true. Cleo brings out the worst in me, she argued to herself, but that's because she's treating Robert badly and I'm on his side. Well, Talbot's opinion of her was completely unimportant. She was only an assistant he'd picked up to help him with his current dig.

CHAPTER SEVEN

DURING most of the next day Antonia felt frustrated and irritable. The day was warm and the studio stuffy. By evening she was of the opinion that she had wasted her time after all. Her work dissatisfied her; the tones were all wrong, the colours muddy and drab, even the perspective seemed awry. She might just as well have gone to bathe at the Lido. Morever, Francesca had been out since the unprecedented early hour of ten o'clock and Antonia had been reduced to muttering aloud and scolding herself for her painting mistakes.

She dumped the unfinished pictures in a corner, packed up her easel and returned to the *albergo* to clean herself up, then perhaps join Ingrid and Sven if they were in Perugia and had not gone elsewhere for the day.

At the café where she dined, there was no one she knew, and after a solitary meal she went to the Margharita and down to the store-room. Perhaps a little intricate work on piecing the vases and pots together might soothe her irritations.

She hoped most fervently that Cleo was out enjoying herself and would not suddenly appear. A few ironic or tempestuous remarks from her would stretch Antonia's patience to the limit.

The time slipped by and it was quite late when Antonia returned the store-room key to the porter's desk.

Robert stood idly in the entrance. "Hallo!" he greeted her in surprise. "I thought you'd gone with the others to the San Giovanni Lido to splash about."

The others, she noted. So Talbot had evidently joined Cleo's party, whoever else that contained.

"No, I've been painting today," she replied evenly. "Now I've spent a little time on the jigsaws."

"When is your godfather coming?"

"Towards the end of the week. Thursday, I believe. He'll let us know."

Robert smiled. "Then I suppose you'll be off sightseeing with him?"

"Yes. A few days here, then Florence, possibly Pisa, too."

"When Mr. Canford returns home, what then? Will you come back and work on Talbot's archaeology project, or are you tired of that?"

She smiled and shook her head. "I can't make any plans yet. I don't know. I may come back. I'm not sure."

"I shall be sorry if you go for good," he said, his dark eyes warm with friendliness.

"So shall I," she returned. "I've come to love Perugia and I've learned a tremendous lot about painting here, mostly thanks to you."

"I wish I could have done more."

"You found me an expert to give me candid opinions and then a part of a studio where I could work without upsetting everyone else in the *albergo* with the smell of paint. What more could I ask?"

He gave a quiet laugh, then added. "You've been quite a help where Cleo's concerned."

Immediately the geniality of her mood vanished. She supposed it was too much to hope that Robert could omit Cleo from his conversation for long, especially when he was tied to his work and she was off somewhere amusing herself.

"In what way have I helped?" she forced herself to ask.

"Several. You've been a steadying influence on her. Through you she's widened her interests. The last thing I ever thought she'd take up was archaeology."

Antonia dared not look at Robert. How blind could men be? Did he really believe that Cleo would have bothered if Talbot Drury had not been the director? Widening her interests did not so much include the arts and sciences as the men who were connected with them, Antonia thought uncharitably.

"She's also done some work down in the store-room," Robert continued, "playing with the jigsaws. Very strange! I feel I've still a lot to learn about Cleo."

Antonia could echo that statement. Robert had not even begun to understand one-tenth of the girl's motives and ambitions, her strategy and method of operating.

It was mid-week before Antonia went to work in the store-room. Tomorrow Philip would arrive and then she would have no further opportunity for several weeks.

One glance at the table showed that some intruder

had been at work. Where Antonia had carefully match-
ed shape and colour in adjacent fragments, totally alien
pieces had been inserted. Two other "paper pattern"
designs nearly completed had been scattered as though
someone had deliberately shuffled the pieces as one
might a set of dominoes.

She remembered Robert's admiring remark. "She's
also done some work down in the store-room." But
that was before Sunday. This mischief had been committed since then. Was she suspecting Cleo unjustly?

Antonia sat down on a packing case. Why waste her
time on this work for someone else to destroy?

The door opened and Talbot came in.

"Oh, Antonia, I wanted to see you." His face and
tone of voice were equally grim. "Robert told me you
were down here."

She raised her face and waited. Let him voice his
reasons first, then she would make her own protests.

He looked at her, then glanced away. "It's no good
doing a job half-heartedly. That only leads to confusion. It's considerable help to the man who assembles
the pottery if he has all the available pieces to hand,
but not if they've been carelessly put together."

"And I suppose I'm the inefficient worker?" she
queried in a dangerously calm voice.

"Well, look at this example." He pointed to the
table. "It must be obvious to you that one piece doesn't
match another."

"It's certainly obvious," she agreed, "but—" She
had been going to say that someone else had tampered
with the assembled bits, or else accidentally scattered
them. His next words infuriated her.

"Cleo has managed to put together two excellent examples, practically complete except for a few small
particles. If she can do it, why can't you? I thought
your sense of artistry was better than that."

Antonia almost choked. So Cleo had passed off Antonia's careful work as her own!

"What were the numbers of the pots?" she asked
brusquely.

Every paper design bore a number corresponding with each group of fragments.

"I can't say now because the man who does the cementing has taken them away for a special drying process."

"They were Numbers 29 and 36," she said firmly.

"How can you be sure?" he asked.

"Because I— Because—oh, what does it matter?" How could she accuse Cleo of this mischief without real proof? Talbot would merely believe that she was trying to dodge the blame. She controlled her raging temper and said as calmly as possible, "I promise I won't interfere again. I'll leave the job to Cleo."

When she reached the door of the store-room she said, "Will you lock up when you've finished and return the key to the porter? I wouldn't like to be held responsible for having left the place unlocked."

She was seething with rage as she left the hotel and went out into the street. He had not even started by asking for explanations. No, he had to accuse her of inefficiency right away. She had probably burned her boats completely over the excavation site, as well as the jigsaw assembly, for she would not go there voluntarily and Talbot would certainly not invite her.

She walked through the little back streets of the city, hardly caring about the direction until, descending a narrow alley and a flight of steps, she found herself close to the Etruscan Arch. She sat on the stone bench at the foot of the arch and scarcely heard the traffic speeding by. She was furious with herself because this man had the power to hurt her. If anyone else had been involved, for instance, Robert, she would have been able to explain without even accusing Cleo, but passing off the situation as an accidental upsetting of the fragments.

But she found it impossible to reason with Talbot. She could scarcely believe that he was the same man with whom she had shared the day of the Feast of the Candles at Gubbio, even though that had ended in an irritating anti-climax with the intrusion of Cleo.

121

Gradually she became more tranquil, or perhaps it was the influence of the old arch above her, spreading its silent peace on her. How many hasty entries and exits, broken appointments had been witnessed by this old gate? Lovers parting after a stormy scene, families fleeing from the wrath of some nobleman's bodyguard, invading men-at-arms bursting through the gate to seize the city.

As she regained her sense of proportion she was now aware of the presence of another occupant of the stone bench. For a leaping instant she wondered if Talbot had followed her, perhaps to apologise, but one discreet glance showed her the face of a smiling Italian.

After a minute or so she rose unhurriedly and walked along the road to the Piazza Fortebraccio. To give any appearance of haste would have been an invitation for the man to follow her.

When Phillip arrived next day an informal dinner-party had been arranged for him at the Margharita by Robert, so that he could meet Cleo and her mother and Talbot.

During the general conversation Antonia caught one or two veiled glances from Talbot, enigmatic looks that she preferred not to decipher, and as he was seated at the far end of the table, there was luckily no opportunity of a whispered word or two.

To her surprise, Talbot cordially invited Philip to visit the excavation site whenever he chose or had time. "Antonia knows exactly where it is."

So this was Talbot's way of crooking his finger and beckoning her again to the site, but she vowed she would not go again except to accompany Philip.

"What a handsomely distinguished man your godfather turns out to be!" exclaimed Cleo to Antonia when the two girls happened to be alone. "I imagined an old greybeard doddering about."

Antonia smiled. "Godfathers come in all ages, as well as shapes and sizes. They don't have to conform to the intervals between the generations."

For the next three or four days Antonia's time was

occupied in accompanying Philip on sightseeing excursions to neighbouring towns or wandering about Perugia itself. Antonia took him to her studio and displayed her work.

"None of it very good, I'm afraid," she observed, "but I'm slowly learning how to improve it."

"Why have you stayed so long in one place?" asked Philip, studying a painting showing part of the Priors' Palace and the Great Fountain.

"Several reasons, I suppose. Learning Italian in what is said to be the best university for foreigners in Europe. Then I was roped in to make sketches for the excavations."

"And when do you contemplate moving on?"

"Oh, quite soon. Any time, in fact," she replied quickly.

"Don't you want to see the results of Talbot Drury's dig?"

"I might come back and look if there's anything exciting."

Philip chose to visit the excavations on the following Monday. He had brought his own car and Antonia directed him to the main part of the site. Stefano hurried to meet them, explaining that Talbot was not available for the time being, but might shortly return.

He conducted Philip over the various sections, pointing out where various small finds had been made. Then Talbot returned and greeted Philip.

"Bad news, I'm afraid," he said to Antonia. "Either some rival team of archaeologists has heard about Luciano and the possibilities under his house, or casual robbers are out to find what they can."

"What's happened?" she queried.

"We've found evidence of the beginning of a tunnel under the house. The two young children were playing about and found they could jump up and down happily on a piece of corrugated iron until it suddenly slipped sideways and shot one child down a hole in the ground."

"Was the child injured?"

"Only a bruise or so and a few cuts. The boy was more frightened than hurt, I expect. The older girls pulled him out, then one of them came to tell us."

"But Luciano wasn't at home?" Antonia asked.

"No. Naturally he's at work."

"D'you suspect anyone belonging to the site? Or has Luciano sold out to someone else, d'you think?"

Talbot's face was thoughtful. "I don't know—yet. What would the Pontellis gain from anyone else that they couldn't get from me?"

"More money?"

He nodded. "Possibly. But I have the authorities on my side and I've now received the permits. So it's obvious that other tunnel-makers are working illegally."

"What will you do now?"

"Start work at once with or without Luciano's permission. Then, of course, we can put a guard or night-watchman on."

"Supposing someone bribes the night-watchman?" suggested Philip, who had been standing close by.

Talbot laughed. "An everyday risk."

Then across the sloping hillside Luciano appeared. He explained that Martina had come to fetch him because of the accident to his small brother.

"Let's all sit down," Talbot suggested. "Don't go, Antonia," he called as she and Philip began to move away out of earshot. "Luciano must have witnesses, too. Antonia, perhaps you could bring Signora Pontelli and Martina here."

When Luciano's mother and elder sister accompanied Antonia back to the group, Stefano was also there and several of the workmen from the site.

Talbot spoke to Luciano of his plans and then flourished the government permits. "What is your answer, Luciano?" he asked.

The boy looked first at Talbot, then at Stefano and the other Italians. When they nodded, he said, "Yes, I will agree."

Martina gave a wild excited laugh at the thought, no doubt, of riches to come, but her mother merely said

"*Buon giorno*" to the collective company and then returned to her cooking.

Talbot told Luciano that proper legal documents would be prepared and that he would receive part of the money almost immediately.

Antonia said impulsively, "And I will buy you a camera for a present, Luciano. Then you can make your own photographs of all the discoveries."

The boy's face lit with pleasure. "*Grazie, signorina*," he said shyly, all truculence vanished, but that perhaps was because today she was wearing a smart dress and not the grubby working clothes she used on the site.

Eventually Philip and Antonia decided it was time to leave.

"If you're going up towards Gubbio," Talbot said to Antonia, "you could lunch at that restaurant where we went on the Candles day. It's about the best. D'you remember where it was?"

"I think I can find it," she replied. Almost every detail of that day was imprinted on her mind.

"Sorry I can't accompany you both," he apologised, "but I've a crowded programme here."

In the car while Philip drove as she directed, Antonia was thoughtful. She remembered that Martina's boy-friend of the moment was one of Talbot's workmen. Was there some connection there with the attemp to tunnel from another point?

She spoke to Philip and gave him the outline of the situation. "Martina's desperate for money, although I think she'd be quite willing to earn some. She even sold her hair."

"She'd be much more likely to make it easy for her young man to start hacking his way through from the basement or cellars of the house, instead of tunnelling from what may be a misguided point on the hillside."

"And of course, without proper safeguards the house might collapse about the family's ears."

In Gubbio, Antonia told Philip about the *festa* to which Talbot had brought her and the exciting race of the candle-like structures, but she chose a different restaurant from the one that Talbot had recommended and refused to ask herself the reason.

"How about going off to Florence in a day or two?" Philip suggested. "No hurry. We can fit it in with whatever you want to do."

The sooner the better, thought Antonia, but she did not say the words so baldly. "All I want to do is buy Luciano a camera, a fairly simple one that will take good pictures. Then when he's learned some technique, he can progress to a more expensive affair."

Philip helped her to choose the camera in Perugia's best shop, which happened to be near the delightful chocolate store.

"That smell must simply charm money from people's pockets," he said, "on the principle that aromas that float out must surely entice the customers in."

"Delicious chocolates, too," Antonia commented.

After the camera purchase, Philip bought two large presentation boxes of Perugina chocolates for Antonia and Cleo, for delivery to their respective hotels. At the travel agents' Philip arranged in advance for hotel accommodation for himself and Antonia.

Before dinner that evening, Antonia was sitting in the entrance hall of the Margharita, when Philip's gift box of chocolates arrived at the desk and Cleo appeared at that moment asking for letters. She took the box from the page, noticed Antonia and walked over to her.

"Isn't it divine? The way Talbot keeps sending me these marvellous chocolates—I shall put on no end of weight, if I'm not careful."

Antonia smiled complacently. "I had an almost identical box delivered to me today." She watched Cleo's face. "I think on this occasion you'll find a card from my godfather inside the wrappings."

To Antonia's surprise, Cleo burst into delighted laughter and sat next to her on the settee. "I'm beginning to have a great respect for you, Antonia," she said. "No chance of hoodwinking you."

"It's always more difficult with one's own sex," replied Antonia, aware that this was not at all true where Cleo was concerned.

"Exactly. Even some men are more difficult than others."

"Which ones have you found so troublesome?" asked Antonia with an innocent gleam in her eyes.

Cleo laughed again. "D'you think I'd tell you? In any case, defeat doesn't last with me. I usually manage to overcome resistance."

After Cleo had gone on the pretext of finding her mother, Antonia wondered why this sudden show of friendship.

When Philip appeared, Antonia said. "Your chocolates were much appreciated, in all directions."

He began to chuckle. "I hope that little baggage was properly mystified. I put in a plain card with the words "From a devoted admirer." She'll be convinced that she's made another conquest."

Antonia laughed shamefacedly. "I'm afraid I've spoilt your joke. I let it out that they were from you."

"Capital!" he exclaimed. "She'll think no fool like an old fool. Come on, Tonia, let's have dinner. I'm hungry after all this chocolate talk."

Antonia had a great deal to do next day packing up her painting gear at the studio to leave it as tidy as possible, sorting out the clothes she wanted to take to Florence and settling her account at the *albergo*, but she still found time to get Philip to run her out to the excavation site so that she could give Luciano his camera.

He had just come home from his work in the vineyards and his gratitude was touching. His face lit with pleasure as he fingered the shining chromium parts, held it at eye-level and viewed the landscape in a wide arc.

Antonia told him how to operate the camera, pointed out the printed instruction booklet. "Stefano will probably show you exactly how to make good pictures."

When she returned to the car and Philip and finally

waved to Luciano, she said, "How little it costs to give a young boy such pleasure! I was afraid if I offered it too soon, he'd think it was a bribe."

On the leisurely drive next day towards Florence, Philip suggested stopping for lunch at San Gimignano. "I seem to remember vaguely a square with a well in the middle."

"That's it. The Piazza of the Cistern," Antonia supplied. "A huge cobbled square surrounded by very old buildings and several of the tall brick towers at one corner."

After an excellent meal at the main café in the square, Phillip and Antonia explored the outskirts of the town, where excavations were in progress most of the time.

"It amazes me that as many of these old fortress towers still remain," remarked Antonia, as she and Philip looked back towards the town. "They're like elegant factory chimneys, only considerably larger, of course."

"They certainly made good lookouts to view the approaching enemy," agreed Philip.

Philip declared his intention of doing the sights of Florence at a leisurely pace. "I gave myself mental indigestion when I came here years ago, mixing up one cathedral with another, so that in the end I'd virtually seen nothing of importance."

Antonia laughed. "Oh, I'm with you entirely. I realise that if one is here for only three or four days, you have to make a great effort to see some things and leave out others."

"This time we can potter and saunter together. What we don't visit one day we can do another."

Their hotel faced a pleasant little square of garden where children played and students strolled or sat on stone benches in the shade. The hotel also possessed a walled garden with lime trees and a towering palm, and most of the visitors took all their meals at tables in the open.

Very soon, one of the waiters explained, the sun

would be too hot at midday and lunch would be served in a cool, air-conditioned restaurant.

"Even the climate manages to let you enjoy yourself," Antonia said one morning at breakfast. "Can you imagine having even coffee and rolls in the middle of an English garden in June? There'd probably be a nippy wind or it'd be raining."

Philip smiled. "I'm beginning to wonder if I've done the right thing for you, Antonia, after all. Giving you this little taste of life in a warm climate may have altered your whole outlook on the future."

"For the better, I hope," she answered, laughing. "I shall at least ·be able to look back on one splendid summer." She picked up a letter she had received this morning from her mother. "Read what Mother says about 'flaming June' in England. They're in the midst of a cold spell with icy rain, gales and hailstorms. Let me enjoy my little spell of *La Dolce Vita*!"

Between visits to the art galleries and museums so that Antonia could renew her acquaintance with the Florentine masters, she and Philip spent pleasant afternoons walking over the bridges to the south side of the Arno to stroll in the Boboli gardens or climb up to the Forte Belvedere and look across the river at most of Florence spread out for inspection.

They viewed from all sides the Ponte Vecchio, restored after the disastrous floods of a year or so back when the Arno wrecked the goldsmiths' and jewellers' shops on the bridge, then tore through the city creating unprecedented havoc to palaces and humble shops alike, to statues and frescoes and the cobbled streets themselves.

"What a colossal amount of work everyone must have put in to re-create what was here before," murmured Antonia as she turned the corner of a street where a marble tablet recorded the flood level, nearly eighteen feet.

"I can't help thinking," she continued, "that if this kind of damage had happened at home, the old bridge would have been replaced with a nice tidy structure of concrete and steel."

"And where would they have put that secret corridor that connected the Uffizi with the Pitti Palace across the river?" asked Philip. "It had to go over the bridge somewhere."

"Yes, I know. It doesn't need much imagination to conjure up what shocking deeds might have been done down there, what secret assignations, whispered intrigues. In sixteenth-century Florence you never knew when your enemy might be lurking around the next corner, ready with his sword at your throat."

Antonia and Philip both had a liking for market places and spent hours pottering among the stalls. Antonia found a beautiful purse tooled intricately in gold on dark green leather.

"Mother will love this," she said to Philip. "D'you think you could take it home for her when you go?"

"Of course. I'll take it with my own odds and ends."

During the few days that she had been in Florence with Philip, Antonia had found more peace and serenity than she had known during the last few weeks in Perugia. It was restful to be far away from Talbot's variable moods and Cleo's mischievous chatter. Perhaps when Philip resumed his business visits and finally returned to England, she would change her plans. She could go back to Perugia for a day or so to collect the rest of her belongings, then go to Rome and Naples. So far she had seen only a tourist's-eye view of Rome, and nothing at all of Naples and farther south. She owed it to Philip to visit as many parts of Italy as possible.

It was ironical that she should be thinking these thoughts as she dressed for dinner one evening and then went out to join Philip in the hotel garden, only to find Cleo and Mrs. Norwood at an adjacent table.

Inevitably, Philip suggested that, with Mrs. Norwood's permission, the tables might be joined together. Cleo looked radiant in a pale shell pink dull satin dress trimmed with crystal beadwork. As usual Mrs.

Norwood was elegant in a plain stone colour dress with dark mink at the neck, and wearing the most fascinating earrings, swinging clusters of jewel flowers with the lily of Florence as a centre.

"We came today," explained Mrs. Norwood, "because Robert told us that in a day or so there's a football match in one of the squares." She laughed. "Of course I wasn't in the least interested. I'm certainly no football fan, but he said this was quite an event, in sixteenth-century costume and floodlit and so on. So we thought we'd better not miss it."

"Yes, we saw some spectator stands being erected in the Piazza della Signoria," Philip told her. "We must get seats for this affair."

Antonia viewed with some distaste the prospect of spending the rest of her time in Florence as one of an ill-assorted quartet. No doubt Philip and Mrs. Norwood could be amiable companions, but what sort of compatibility could she and Cleo find in being together? Yet Cleo was in her friendliest mood without the slightest hint of veiled antagonism. Antonia wondered if the cause lay in the fact that neither Robert nor Talbot were here in Florence.

Mrs. Norwood and the two girls spent a couple of mornings shopping and window-gazing in the Via Tornabuoni, the Bond Street of Florence, where shops set out their leatherwork, handbags, shoes, embroidery and fashions with an air of aristocratic dignity, as though every shop were owned by a princess, no less.

The Norwoods bought a couple of dresses each and some elegant shoes; Antonia contented herself with a hand-embroidered blouse.

Philip had apparently secured seats for the football match, the *Giuoco del Calcio* in costume, and after a fairly early dinner, the four took a taxi to the nearest point to the Piazza that traffic was allowed.

The Piazza della Signoria was transformed. The vast space was floodlit, the high crenellated tower edged with pin-point diamonds of light against a blue-black sky.

With bands playing and banners flying, contingents of men in sixteenth-century costume began to march into the centre arena, some groups in blue and red striped doublets and hose, others in white or yellow or red, according apparently to which part of the city they belonged. They formed glittering patterns of colour, then they retreated to form a border against the red-draped boards behind which thousands of spectators sat tier above tier.

Antonia had never been particularly interested in football and knew little of the general method of play, much less the finer points, but when the match began even she could see that the game was not the sort that took place at Wembley.

The players seemed to number about fifty instead of twenty-two, the rough artificial turf that had been spread to cushion their falls was kicked about more than the ball and the method of scoring goals was quite baffling to Antonia since there were apparently no goal-posts. Only the shouts and cheers of the spectators confirmed when a goal was scored.

It was altogether a gay zany spectacle and she thought that a few football matches like this would liven up English soccer no end, although the *Calico* was obviously much older than the modern kind of football.

For some few minutes she had been aware that someone had taken the vacant seat next to her, but she was so absorbed in the game that she had not turned her head to notice. When a man's hand gently closed over one of hers she turned sharply, dragging her hand away at the same time, and found herself staring into Talbot's floodlit face.

"Talbot!" she exclaimed. "How did you——" but the rest of her sentence was drowned in a wild burst of cheering as another goal was scored and the players jumped in the air and embraced each other.

"I'm glad I managed to get here in time," he whispered close to her ear. "I wouldn't have missed this for anything."

"But you have missed part of it, all the preliminary marching and so on."

"They do the same thing after the match."

Philip leaned forward in his seat to greet Talbot, but apparently neither Mrs. Norwood nor Cleo had seen him yet.

When play was resumed, Talbot said, "I suppose you don't fancy betting on the result?"

She shook her head and laughed. "I wouldn't know which colour to choose. There seem to be so many."

"Wise of you," he murmured. "Never bet unless you can clearly see the runners."

"Many people stick a pin in a list of horses or teams. How about that?"

"True," he conceded. "Perhaps they have just as much luck as those on the course."

For the rest of the match Antonia's attention was divided between the extraordinary game in front of her and a sense of elation that Talbot was close beside her. Philip must have known that he was coming otherwise the extra seat would not have been booked, but who had manipulated the seating so that the vacant place was next to Antonia and not Cleo?

In a way she was reminded of that day at Gubbio, the Feast of the Candles, but would history repeat it—and Cleo claim him?

After the match the festivities were apparently not over, for after the last group of costumed men had marched out in the wake of the triumphant players, whichever side that was, the Piazza was darkened and fireworks soared from every possible rooftop, piercing the dark sky with glittering splashes of coloured light.

Finally the entertainment came to an end and the spectators slowly left the stands. Only now did Talbot greet Mrs. Norwood and Cleo. Mrs. Norwood's greeting in return was so cool that Antonia suspected that she had known for some time that he was among the party. Cleo's expression gave nothing away. She neither smiled nor frowned, nor even seemed surprised.

This time Antonia need not have feared that Talbot would abandon her for Cleo, as Philip suggested that all the party should have supper at one of the expensive restaurants in the Via Tornabuoni.

"Where are you staying?" Mrs. Norwood asked Talbot during the meal.

"On the other side of the Arno. Near the Piazza Santo Spirito." He glanced across the table at Cleo. "From that side you get the best views of the city."

Cleo smiled almost mechanically and nodded agreement.

Antonia felt she was floundering out of her depth. Her elation had already faded, for it seemed to her that Talbot had not come to Florence for a particular festivity date in the calendar, but in order to be near Cleo.

His next words did not clarify the situation, but threw a cloak of dissimulation over his real purpose. "I wanted to visit the Archaeological Museum here again, particularly the Etruscan exhibits. I also have one or two officials to meet in connection with our own excavations."

Mrs. Norwood shot him a sceptical glance, which Antonia interpreted as one of disbelief in the professional purpose of his visit.

In a way, Antonia was relieved that Talbot was at least not staying in the same hotel as herself and Cleo. Thus she would be spared the sight of watching them together or knowing that they were out somewhere in each other's company.

In her room as she prepared for bed, Antonia peered at her reflection in the mirror, forcing herself to answer why she should be so irritated, her feelings so ruffled because Talbot had followed Cleo. Well, there was Robert to consider. Did he know where Talbot was? Oh, it was very discreet of Talbot to choose an hotel on the far side of the river, but bridges were made for crossing and there were plenty of those in Florence.

As Antonia expected, now that Talbot had arrived, Cleo and her mother made their own sightseeing arrangements, leaving Philip and Antonia as free as when they first came.

A couple of days after the football match, Antonia and Philip went again to Fiesole. They had already visited the Roman theatre and baths, but today they saw in the Franciscan church an exhibition of Chinese treasures collected by one of the monks.

As they descended the steep hill, then stopped at the cafe halfway down for coffee and cakes, Philip spoke of Talbot and his work.

"Is he really a dedicated archaeologist?" he asked.

Antonia paused for a moment before replying. "I think so. He means to make it his life work, I believe."

"You don't sound too sure about it," Philip teased her.

"How can I be? I don't really know what's in the man's mind."

"I thought you knew just that. Is the young Cleo smitten with him?"

Antonia smiled. "It's always hard to say that at any given time. She's supposed to be almost engaged to Robert, yet she flirts with anyone who seems likely to respond. It's all fun to her."

"So he's come to Florence to chase Cleo. Is that it?"

"I take it so," she replied.

"Or has he come to chase you, Antonia?"

She turned to Philip. "I'm the last person he would chase, as you so inelegantly put it. He's probably out somewhere now with Cleo. I doubt if he's stewing in the museums."

"You're wrong. He isn't in the museum and he hasn't Cleo tagging along, for here he comes now."

Talbot waved a salute as he mounted the flight of steps to the little terraced tea-garden. "Sorry to be rather late," he said.

Antonia glared speechlessly and accusingly at her godfather. What put-up job was this?

With Talbot apologising for delay, it was obvious that both he and Philip had arranged some kind of appointment. But for whose benefit? After Talbot had been sitting for some time and Philip had ordered more coffee and cakes, it occurred to her that the two men were engaged in a lengthy discussion of topics ranging from the beauties of Florence to the price of small properties in the hills, the delicious golden mushrooms and the fact that the young women and girls of Siena were so often fair-haired with delicate features like paintings by medieval artists.

Eventually Philip rose. "I wonder if you'd mind, Antonia, but I promised some friends of mine who have a villa close by that when I was up this way I'd call for the evening and take dinner with them. You and Talbot, no doubt, can find something to do with your time. It's a pleasant walk down to the river or probably Talbot knows the country lanes around here and can find a rustic *trattoria* where you can eat a superb meal in quiet surroundings."

Her instinct was to return at once to Florence alone and by any route that offered, rejecting Talbot's company entirely, but as Philip called "*Arrivederci*" and moved towards the steps, there was a look in Talbot's eyes that was both challenging and coolly sardonic. It seemed as though he was daring her to say, "Thanks very much, but I'd rather find my own way back to Florence."

Instead she gave him a wavering smile. "So you're apparently saddled with me whether you like it or not, but if you have other arrangements for this evening, please go ahead. I won't mind."

He leaned in his chair with one arm thrown over the back of it. "Why are you so prickly?"

"I don't think it's being prickly to allow you a graceful way of getting out of an unlooked-for dinner engagement."

"And supposing I don't need these graceful excuses?" he queried.

"Possibly you don't like eating alone in your hotel and even my company is better than solitude."

He began to laugh, then shook his head. "Sometimes I think you positively dislike me very much and at others you school yourself to tolerate me. What's so detestable about me?"

"I've never said or thought anything of the kind, but you wouldn't care for it if I were to start analysing your character, all the bad and the good."

He tilted his chair back and forth. "You mean my vices would make too long a catalogue?"

"Your virtues might be too short a list to be worth mentioning," she retorted.

"Charity is not one of your virtues, Antonia," he said, "but let's go now. We're wasting time when we could at least be admiring the scenery on our way down to the city."

As they wandered through dense olive groves and vineyards past superb villas, her resentment vanished both against Philip for his rather clumsy manoeuvre and Talbot for his cool acceptance of it. Sunset lent a golden radiance to the whole landscape, the russet rooftops glowed with a fiery red and the deep black of cypresses became tinged with brown. The distant mountains of Vallombrosa became dark purple and the plains, grey-green or misty blue, were punctuated by the towers of castles or the pale walls of patrician villas.

"Oh, if only I could paint such a scene in all its richness!" murmured Antonia, as she and Talbot had paused to watch this short sunset interval between the daytime brilliance and violet-dark night.

"You must make up your mind whether to paint the landscape or capture it on colour film," Talbot said softly.

"What a Philistine!" she jeered gently. "How could you say this in Florence of all cities?"

He grinned. "If you can think of anything so mundane as food, we could have dinner at this rustic *trattoria* as Mr. Canford suggested. It's only a few yards away."

"Thoughtful of you both. I begin to think that this evening was most carefully planned by the pair of you."

"And why should that displease you?" he demanded.

"It doesn't." She turned towards him and laughed.

He took her arm and together they went towards the small restuarant. Today it was so easy to enjoy Talbot's company provided she did not allow his nearness to magnify those faint, ridiculous hopes that crept sometimes across her mind. Always she must remember that he had declared that he would not clutter his life with women. If he changed his mind about that, then it was Cleo with whom he would choose to be cluttered.

But tonight she yielded to the dream that Talbot might always be this gay, happy companion, choosing the exotic dishes offered by a voluble restaurant proprietor, raising his glass of deliciously dry white wine, talking of his hopes that one day he might have the luck of a really resounding discovery of importance.

Then the descent home in the quiet darkness spangled by fireflies and the silences broken only by the liquid melody of nightingales from every tree.

They walked through the long, narrow streets where overhanging eaves of old palaces seemed to lean towards each other, casting deep shadows. Massive stone coats of arms were set high above the portals and there were glimpses of dimly-lit courtyards with wrought iron gates and enormous metal lanterns.

"I believe this part of Florence is even more romantic than the other side of the river," she murmured.

"It has its own character here on the south bank, the same as the left bank in Paris."

It struck her that his tone had suddenly cooled. Was it because of her careless use of the word "romantic?" She must be more discreet or he would imagine that she was taking a leaf out of Cleo's book and trying to flirt with him.

She became silent, racking her brains for the least provocative topic. Then in the shadow of a group of trees surrounding the Piazzale Michelangelo, he seized her hand, swung her towards him and kissed her full on the mouth.

She was too surprised to respond and the moment was so fleeting that it might never have happened.

"I've wanted to do that for quite a while," he said. "I thought you were feeling in a romantic mood, but I gather I was mistaken. Forgive me."

As they walked on she tried to compose her feelings, then said, "I was surprised, that's all."

"There are moments when I'm almost human, in spite of the fact that Cleo calls me 'Dreary Drury.' But let's forget it, shall we?"

"Of course." But she found that she did not want to forget the tiny incident. Her mind was busy, too, over the disclosure of Cleo's nickname for him. Was he "Dreary Drury" when he didn't respond quickly enough to her provocative wiles?

When they reached the Piazza Santo Spirito, Talbot asked, "Are you tired? D'you want a taxi home?"

She hesitated. His hotel was on this side of the river. If he put her into a taxi he could be rid of her, as it were, after an anti-climax ending to a carefully arranged evening. So, perversely, she declared that she was not at all tired. "I'd rather walk," she said, knowing that he would not allow her to go back to her hotel alone.

They sat for a while drinking coffee at a pavement café in the square in front of the fountain, then walked across the Santa Trinita bridge, along the streets with brilliantly-lit windows, so different from the darkened narrow streets of the south bank. They talked of their impressions of Florence, compared one church with another, spoke of frescoes and sculptures, markets and galleries, just like a pair of tourists who happened to be staying in the city at the same time. All the warm companionship, the pleasant harmony had vanished from their relationship, and Antonia blamed herself. Why could she not have accepted a lighthearted kiss in the spirit in which it was probably meant? Why make a fuss as though she had never been kissed before in the shade of a tree? But she knew the real answer. Somewhere along the path of her association with Talbot, since the beginning of his work at Perugia, she had allowed herself to become too deeply involved in a desire for his approval of all she did. She did not want a kiss or two to keep her sweet-tempered and in the right frame of mind to rush up to the excavation site whenever he beckoned. She knew that she wanted a great deal more than this, but she refused to define in her mind a single wisp of aspiration or ambition. She would not try to look into the future in case the prospect might be too bleak to bear.

CHAPTER EIGHT

PHILIP had a couple of business calls to make in Florence next day and when Antonia returned to the hotel for lunch she found Mrs. Norwood alone at their table in the garden.

"Cleo is out somewhere," Mrs. Norwood explained. "Said she'd probably not be in to lunch."

Antonia studied the menu and ordered a meal.

After a few minutes, Mrs. Norwood said quietly, "I'm glad we've this little opportunity for a chat."

Antonia waited.

"I'm rather worried about Cleo," the older woman began. "I thought the arrangement between her and Robert was quite definitely settled. I know that he's reliable enough. He's tremendously fond of her, but Cleo—" Mrs. Norwood broke off and shook her head sadly. "If it were a case of being attracted to almost every man she meets, I wouldn't worry. That's fairly natural at her age, and I have every confidence that in a year, perhaps, she'd settle down with Robert very happily indeed."

"What is it that makes you anxious?" queried Antonia, more for something to say in punctuation and not because she was unaware of what was coming.

"It's Talbot, of course. Oh, he's a perfectly nice chap. I've nothing against him, except—well, let me put it this way. Robert's prospects are considerable. I understand that his father has made some new business merger which increases his fortune and whenever Robert chooses to give up that rather ridiculous job at the hotel, he can return to England and direct and control a dozen companies."

"And of course, you want Cleo to share Robert's brilliant future." Antonia spoke quietly and without sarcasm.

"Naturally. Cleo is our only child and her father and I have done all we could to give her the right background. We're not poor. It could be said that we're moderately well off, but I doubt whether Cleo will ever have the chance of such a good match as Robert. That is, if she foolishly lets Robert go."

"D'you believe that's her intention?"

Mrs. Norwood sighed. "I don't know what to believe. Talbot has been far too attentive to her for my peace of mind. He seems to have followed us here at the earliest date he could get away from his excavations. I'm never sure whether she's out with him or not. Today, for instance, they may have gone out for the day together. Certainly last night I think she skipped off to have dinner with him."

Antonia gasped. What was she to say now? Tell Mrs. Norwood the truth or, by implication, cast suspicion that Cleo was out with someone entirely different?

She took the coward's way and remained silent, fearful of entangling herself in a situation that was complex enough already.

"So I thought you could help me, Antonia," Mrs. Norwood was saying.

"In what way?"

"By taking Talbot off Cleo's hands, as it were. Oh, I know this sounds rather crude, but I'm almost desperate. He's started giving her expensive presents."

Antonia glanced up quickly at Cleo's mother. "But Cleo doesn't want to accept them?"

"I've insisted on her returning them, of course. But

if while we're all still here, you could—er—divert Talbot from Cleo, I should be so grateful."

Antonia shook her head. "I don't really see what I can do. If Talbot prefers Cleo, then it's no use my trying to come between them, is it? Besides, he might mistake my motives."

Mrs. Norwood smiled. "You mean he might think you were jealous—or running after him?"

"Something like that. In any case, you probably have little to worry about. Talbot can't stay away long from his excavations whether Cleo is here or in Perugia. Why don't you and Cleo go off somewhere else? To Elba or other parts of Italy. Or if you've seen most of this country, you could try Austria or Switzerland. You could easily say that the cooler mountain climate suited you better during hot weather than most of the places here."

"That might be a possible solution, but then it also separates Cleo from Robert. If we could persuade Robert to come along with us, that would really help."

"I couldn't prophesy about that," said Antonia. "You'll have to approach Robert himself."

Mrs. Norwood patted Antonia's hand. "Well, it's been helpful to chat the situation over with you, my dear, and if you could do anything to—to—er—annexe, shall we say?—Talbot for a few weeks, I should appreciate it very much."

Antonia watched Mrs. Norwood walk through the garden to the covered terrace leading to the hotel. Outwardly, elegance itself with never a frown to encourage a wrinkle, the perfectly poised mother of a ravishingly beautiful daughter, yet underneath that tranquillity lay all the maternal hopes and fears that afflicted other women.

So Talbot had now started giving Cleo presents! It seemed clear that he had deliberately followed the Norwoods to Florence to be out of the way of Robert. Then what sort of game was he playing last night, allowing Philip to arrange dinner appointments? The memory of that carelessly bestowed kiss made Antonia writhe with rage mingled with shame. Was it Talbot's idea to throw dust in everyone's eyes to conceal his overwhelming attraction to Cleo, or had Antonia looked and sounded as though she expected a counterfeit titbit of romance in a setting so charged with the trappings of emotion?

Certainly she would be compelled to hint gently to Philip that there must be no more substitute partners for evening engagements. Once was enough of that!

Cleo tapped on Antonia's bedroom door when the latter was dressing for dinner.

"Had a good day?" queried Antonia, carefully omitting the words "with Talbot."

"Marvellous." Cleo flung herself on Antonia's bed. Then she sat up suddenly. "Antonia, could I ask you a favour?"

"You can try."

"It's rather awkward." Cleo twined her long blonde hair round her fingers and her blue eyes became thoughtful.

"What is?"

"Well, you see, I've received the most wonderful present and I don't know what to do about it."

Antonia restrained herself from blurting out that Cleo's mother had already disclosed this piece of news.

"If it's not from Robert, then you'll have to return it, won't you?" she suggested gently.

"You know perfectly well that it couldn't be from Robert," Cleo's blue eyes flashed angrily. "Otherwise there'd be no problem. If I could not really trust you, I'd tell you it was from Talbot."

"Then isn't it?" Antonia swung round on the other girl.

"No, but for my mother's sake, I want you to back me up that Talbot gave me this lovely dressing-case with the most exquisite fittings you've ever seen."

Antonia frowned. "What exactly are you driving at? This gift is from someone else that your mother doesn't know about?"

Cleo swung her legs over the edge of the bed and

her face took on the expression of triumphant conquest.

"He's an Italian count," she said. "He has a *palazzo* up in the hills here and a villa on the coast near Grosseto."

"Are you sure? Or is he just a tourist from Milan spinning a yarn and spending his holiday money lavishly enough even to impress you?" Antonia's tone was severely critical.

"Oh, don't lecture me! My mother can do plenty of that. I know she means well." Cleo rose and roamed about the room restlessly. "But if I'm never going to have any fun, I might as well be dead."

"And what fun are you getting out of this situation with the Italian nobleman?" demanded Antonia.

Cleo laughed. "I might have known you'd sneer, but I'll put up with that. I had to confide in you because you might let the cat out of the bag and that would be dangerous."

"Not half so dangerous as this deception you're playing on your mother."

"All I want you to do is take charge of my lovely present for the time being. Then I can tell my mother I've returned it."

"Cleo!" Antonia's voice rose with shock. "What sort of good relationship are you ever going to maintain with your mother if you deceive her like this over such an unimportant thing as a gift from a casual acquaintance?"

"I don't know that Arnolfo is as casual as that. I rather fancy myself as an Italian Contessa."

Antonia sighed. "I think, Cleo, you'll realise in a very short time that all these little adventures are only trivial compared with Robert."

It was Cleo's turn to sigh heavily. "Robert! Robert! Robert! Morning till night, I have Robert and his immense fortune rammed down my throat."

"Tell me this, then. Are you in love with anyone else apart from Robert? If you are, then tell Robert honestly. Even your mother wouldn't try to push you into a loveless marriage for the sake of money."

"I think falling in love must be very overrated," declared Cleo. "What I like best is going out and about with someone new. How on earth can you visualise a future of getting middle-aged and sitting opposite one another by the fire?"

Antonia laughed. "Well, I'm not much older than you, so I'm not exactly experienced in life, but it's obvious that you've never been in love with anyone yet. When it comes you'll be bowled over and wonder how you could ever have had such silly ideas."

"Is that what happened to you?" queried Cleo, with a slightly mischievous smile.

"No, but I'd like to think it could happen that way." Antonia kept her voice well under control. Cleo's secrets might be safe in Antonia's keeping, but the converse would certainly not be true.

"Then you won't help me?" asked Cleo.

"I'd like to, but how can I? I'll promise not to breathe a word either to your mother or Talbot. Or Robert, too, if it comes to that. But disentangle yourself from this Italian count, whoever he is, or else bring him out in the open, introduce him to your mother and let him take his chance. His status can easily be checked up then—and you might have more hopes of becoming a real Contessa, if that's what you really want and—"

"Oh, what a preachy person you are, Antonia!" Cleo interrupted, jumping up off the bed, on which she had again subsided. "I shall have to manage my affairs myself, I can see. I thought you'd be useful. I suppose you're still feeling sore about Talbot? I can't help it if he's followed me here from Perugia and left his precious digging affair."

"He didn't come wholly on your account, I believe." Antonia smiled. "He had to spend time in the Archaeological Museum here and see officials to check up his work."

Cleo waved a deprecating hand. "Pooh! That was the excuse that was good enough for my mother, but she knows as well as I the real reason why he came."

"Very likely," Antonia agreed casually.

Cleo sauntered from the room.

At dinner that evening, Philip suddenly mentioned Pisa. "Would you like to spend a few days there, Antonia?"

She clutched at the chance like a lifeline. "Very much indeed. I was able to spend only a day or two there during the early weeks of my trip."

"Pisa!" echoed Mrs. Norwood, in the tone of one casting around for new ideas. Oh, don't let her and Cleo come, too, thought Antonia wrathfully, but Cleo's next words settled that.

"We've seen Pisa twice, Mother. Once by daylight and once in the enchanting moonlight, as the guide-books say. Let's stay longer in Florence and really explore it together. We haven't seen half yet."

Mrs. Norwood smiled at her daughter.

Antonia had caught the words "together." Did that mean that the Italian count was to be brought out into the open? Or did "together" also include Talbot?

During the afternoon when Antonia was packing her suitcases, a telephone call came from Philip.

"Talbot's on the phone. He wants to speak to you."

Antonia waited for the connection.

"I hear you're leaving for Pisa," Talbot said.

"Oh, Philip told you, I suppose?"

"Yes, I'm leaving tomorrow, too. I've finished all I can do here at the moment and I'm very anxious to get back to the site. All sorts of things may have happened there."

She made non-committal noises. Then he said, "Well, have a good time in Pisa. See you some time in Perugia, I suppose?"

"Yes, I suppose so. I'll let you know when I'm back there."

The cool little conversation puzzled her. Had he heard or been told about Cleo's new charmer and decided that it was best to leave her alone for the time being?

She and Philip had never seen the Leaning Tower by moonlight and it was an experience not to be missed.

"Astonishing!" murmured Philip softly, as they gazed at the domes and columns gleaming with a magical beauty, sharply outlined against the dark sky. "You don't realise how far the Tower is out of the vertical."

"Especially when they say it started to lean before it was finished building," commented Antonia. "You wonder why they didn't start again, instead of just strengthening it."

"We must climb to the top in daylight tomorrow," suggested Philip. "You can see the Carrara mountains, all solid marble and glistening white as glaciers."

One afternoon Antonia spent several hours making rough sketches of baroque palaces on the banks of the Arno and little unexpected corners of the town where a piece of architecture appealed to her. She found that she needed her own absorbing kind of work to prevent her thoughts from dwelling too much on the affairs of Cleo and Talbot.

When she and Philip returned to Perugia he insisted that she should transfer to the Hotel Margharita instead of going back to the small *albergo*.

"You don't have to worry about the difference in cost," he assured her. "I'll take care of that."

"Thank you. Perhaps for the short time I'm going to be here, the difference won't amount to very much," she said.

"Why? Aren't you going to help Talbot with his excavations again?" he queried.

"I don't know. I doubt if he really needs me there. I thought of going down into southern Italy soon. There's so much that I haven't seen."

Philip gave her a questioning glance, but said no more.

At the Margharita, Antonia found that Robert was extremely despondent about his prospects with Cleo.

"It seems that she can't bear to tear herself from Florence," he grumbled. "I know it's a beautiful city with many interesting sights and entertainments to offer, but what else—or who else—is keeping her there?"

Antonia shook her head. "I've no idea, but couldn't you join her there for a few days?"

"Not at present. We're short-staffed and the other assistant manager is away ill."

"Robert, which is going to be more important to you? Following this kind of career where you're tied to hotel-running and its difficulties? Or paying some real attention to Cleo?"

He frowned. "In a way, I thought I was doing it for Cleo's sake. If I can't be a better business man and know at first hand how concerns should be managed, there'd be all the more comfort for Cleo in due course."

"When she's your wife, I suppose? And you're everlastingly tied up with conferences and air trips and board meetings? Cleo is young and lively. She wants to live now as well as in the future. Go to Florence soon and surprise her, buy her nice presents, send her flowers, take her out to the open-air theatre in the Boboli Gardens, make her feel that you regard her as the centre of your universe."

"But she knows that already," he protested.

Antonia sighed.

"Telling her once that you love her isn't enough. Go on telling her every day. At the present time she could be forgiven for believing that the Margharita is more important to you than she is."

He began to laugh. "You're a powerful ally for Cleo, especially as she hasn't always been too sweet to you." At the sight of Antonia's raised eyebrows, he continued, "Oh, yes, I know one or two small incidents. You took the rap when Talbot blamed you for mixing up the pottery pieces, but I know that she was the culprit. She doesn't mean any real harm, of course, but she has that mischievous streak in her."

"Perhaps only because she's bored."

"All right, you win! I'll try to take a few days off quite soon and join Cleo and her mother."

Talbot was so busy working on the site and particularly the beginning of the tunnel under Luciano's house that he apparently returned to the hotel only to sleep.

Antonia worked most days in the studio shared with Francesca, for Philip had now gone to Naples and Rome on business visits.

The Italian classes had finished for her particular course at the University and her various friends, including Ingrid and Sven, had left Perugia. She would have gone willingly to the excavation site, but Talbot had not invited her and she was certainly not going to push herself in unasked.

But one evening when Talbot returned to the hotel early enough for dinner, he joined Antonia at her table.

"I suppose I may join you?"

"Of course."

After a while he asked. "Did you or Philip give Luciano a camera?"

"Yes. I did."

"I see." His face was sombre.

"Was there anything wrong in that?" she demanded, immediately on the defensive.

"No, not in the gift itself."

"Then in what other way?"

He sighed deeply. "I'm not sure yet. Naturally, the boy is snap-happy, but whether he'd have the skill to take what has apparently been taken, I've no idea. The truth is, Antonia, that when I arrived at Luciano's place two days ago, there was a horde of press photographers and reporters."

"But don't you want publicity?"

"Not yet. Not for some time. Yet the press evidently had quite a bit of information, photographs from an undisclosed source."

"Could it be from one of your men?" Antonia queried.

"It's possible. Someone could say that he'd been instructed by me and Luciano's family would immediately give him whatever facilities he required. It could even be some outsider entirely. We haven't forgotten that a tunnel was being driven from lower down the hillside and one of the small Pontellis fell into it."

"What would anyone have to gain by giving information to the press?" asked Antonia.

"That depends on how much someone wants to cash in on the discoveries we're making."

"I still don't see who would really benefit. How did you handle the press?"

Talbot chuckled. "Told them rather roughly to clear off, I'm afraid. But afterwards I explained that we hadn't anything of importance to show them yet, but we'd let them know as soon as we had."

Antonia smiled. "Your public relations department is not functioning too well, is it?"

"No. Perhaps it's a job you could do?"

"I'm no expert in these matters."

"When are you coming up to the site? Or aren't you interested now?"

"Of course I'm still interested. I didn't know you wanted me there."

He gave her a curious glance, half hostile, half inviting.

"When you've time to spare, you could make yourself useful," he said coolly.

"Then you'll have to arrange transport for me. Philip is away in the South."

When she went to the site two days later Luciano's family, the Pontellis, were moving out their few belongings and carrying them to a bullock-cart. Martina's young man friend, Guido, was there to help with the heavier articles and indulged in a show of horseplay that sent the two older girls into fits of hysterical laughter.

"You have never moved from house before?" queried Antonia of Emilia, the younger.

"No. We know no other house. We were born here."

Luciano was of course away at his work in the vineyards. As head of his house he could not forgo a day's pay to install his family in another residence.

When eventually the cart moved off with the mother and two small children perched among the tables and chairs and mattresses and Martina, Emilia and the young man walking alongside, Antonia asked Talbot, "Are you going to demolish the house straightaway?"

"No, not yet. While it still stands up, it can provide shelter for the tunnelling party and a couple of rooms for the men to use for eating. It's not pleasant to eat your food in a tunnel where anything may fall into your wine or spaghetti."

During most of the day Antonia worked on other parts of the site, where several important finds had recently been made. There were large fragments of what looked like wall plaques, sometimes with inscriptions, and these were carefully photographed, measured, sketched and their situation pin-pointed on the charts.

Towards evening Talbot suggested that she might like to see the start of the tunnel. "It's more or less on our way home, anyway."

They descended into the cellar of Luciano's house. One or two old wine bottles still lay about in the corners. A wall had an aperture large enough for a man to walk through if he bent double or crawled.

"We can't enlarge this hole at the moment," explained Talbot, "or the whole house will fall about our ears and possibly seal us up in our own tunnel, but when we've made a few more yards of progress, then we can knock down most of the wall and it doesn't matter what happens then. We shall have a second escape passage, anyway."

The cellar itself was dry enough, but a dank, musty smell came from the opening of the tunnel. "D'you want to go through?" Talbot asked.

"Of course."

He went first, then held a torch so that she could see where to step. He shone the torch on the roof of the tunnel, showing her the supports, the beams of wood, the metal arches, the steel plates bolted together to form a rough tubular passage.

"I won't take you any farther up there," Talbot said, "because you ought to be wearing a helmet and suitable clothing. Another time."

When they emerged and walked up the path to the car, Antonia said, "Where is the new house the Pontellis have taken?"

"I can show you that in the village as we pass," he promised.

When she saw it, she was both amazed and angry.

"That poor little shack! Why, it's hardly better than the one they've left—or been turned out of!" she exclaimed.

"It's only temporary," Talbot reassured her. "Just for a month or two. Then they'll be able to have one at the other end of the village."

"I should hope so. That place looks about as large as an average cow-shed and just as habitable."

"The Pontellis don't exactly expect all mod. cons.," he snapped, as he drove down the road. "You're taking all this far too seriously."

"I think Luciano and his family haven't been treated very well."

"Look Antonia, it was part of the bargain that the Pontellis should move out on a certain date, regardless of whether tip-top accommodation was available or not. This is the best we can do for the time being, and if you knew the Pontellis, you'd know perfectly well that they're not inclined to spend their money on a luxury house with every amenity. The girls would much rather have a good dowry, all the mother needs is a good cooking stove, and it's possible that Luciano may be able to provide rather better for his small brother and sister than they could hope for."

"It still seems rather like exploiting them. How d'you know they won't go on living in that awful hut for a long time yet?"

"That's their affair," he retorted, his chin taking a stubborn angle, "and not really yours. Why must you make difficulties where none exist?"

For a few miles she remained silent. Then she said,

"I shall go and see them often and persuade them to struggle for that better house elsewhere in the village."

"I wish you luck," he said in the tone of one threatening a malediction.

"I still think you've taken advantage of a young boy's naïveté," she persisted, "but I'll leave the subject alone before you throw me out of the car and leave me to make my own way home."

Callous, she thought. Talbot doesn't care about people or their welfare as long as he gets his own way. The Pontellis are part of the past as far as he is concerned and must fend for themselves.

She was glad not to see Talbot at dinner and thought it likely that he had gone elsewhere for a meal rather than meet her again, although they did not have to share a table. For all Antonia cared, the whole length of the restaurant could be between them.

Robert was off duty by the time she had finished dinner and he came to join her in the courtyard bar.

"My friend Vittorio is in Perugia again," he told her. "Painted any good pictures lately?"

"That depends on the eye of the beholder," she returned. "I hope I've improved and I'd still be glad to have his opinions, however scathing."

"Right. Bring them here on Sunday. He'll look at them in the morning. In the afternoon perhaps we could go to the Lido at Ponte San Giovanni, you and I, that is." Robert laughed. "Vittorio would raise the level of the Lido several inches if he came in swimming!"

Antonia was glad of the diversion. "Yes, I'll come with pleasure. Also perhaps we might visit the Volumni hypogeum. I've been there once, but I feel I should go again now that I know so much more about what to look for."

"Is Talbot hoping to have a rival attraction as good as the Volumni?"

"Yes, I think he is. He deserves it, even if his methods are rugged and hard on people. He'd never think of trampling across his excavation sites in the same ungentle way that he has of handling human beings."

"He's a queer mixture, Antonia," Robert said. "Ruthless where his work and his ambitions are concerned, yet there's a more tolerant side to his nature and sometimes he can be extremely carefree and amusing."

Antonia remained silent, remembering that carefree and amusing moment under the trees across the river in Florence, when it had amused Talbot to kiss her. Perhaps it was his own hard logic, his austere discipline, that caused him to shed his inhibitions for a few light-hearted moments without bothering about the consequences.

Antonia and Robert strolled along the street and eventually returned to the "Perugian balcony" overlooking the wide plain, now twinkling with lights.

When they entered the Margharita again, Talbot rose to join them.

"I've been looking for you, Antonia," he said cheerfully as though there had never been a wrangling word between them only a few hours ago.

"You're not going to start making her work tonight, I hope," put in Robert.

"No, indeed. It occurred to me that—"

"You'll have to excuse me," broke in Robert. "I can see I'm being signalled. Someone is in a panic, no doubt." He hurried off towards the head waiter.

"You were saying?" prompted Antonia coolly.

"Yes, I wondered if you might like to go to the Volumni on Sunday. We might be able to compare the entrances and perhaps the size of the various chambers there, as well as the carvings."

She smiled as she looked him straight in the face. "I'm sorry, Talbot, but Robert has just asked me to go with him."

"On Sunday? Is he off duty, then?"

"So I gather. We shall also go to the Lido for swimming. I have an engagement in the morning, so we can't go until after lunch."

She enjoyed this small triumph as she watched his face cloud over, although the victory was only a petty once. But his arrogance was insufferable. Did he think he could pick her up like a toy and discard her when he chose?

"I see," he said slowly. "Perhaps I may expect you at the site on Monday?"

"If I'm provided with transport, yes. But if you want to leave at a very early hour, no doubt Stefano could give me a lift if you arrange it."

"I'll let you know about that." He turned swiftly and went out of the courtyard, calmly, without apparent anger, but the set of his shoulders and the tilt of his head proclaimed that he was not in one of his carefree or amusing moods.

On Sunday morning Antonia took her best paintings, or at least those she thought most effective, to show to Vittorio. As before, Robert had arranged for the pictures to be exhibited in a suitable room with good lighting, and as Vittorio prowled about, muttering, or drawing in his lips in that well-known gesture which meant failure, Antonia waited expectantly for his verdict.

He gave a sudden smile and it was like the radiance on the face of a saint painted by one of the great Umbrian masters.

"You have learned lessons," he said. "That is good." For a moment she thought he meant the picture he was looking at, but then he said, "This one—a poor thing, but this"—he dashed away to a view of Pisa by the river— "this one glows with light. The reflections in the river are good and there is water there and not muddy land."

He moved away to stand in front of a landscape that showed a wide view of vineyards, rolling plain and distant hills, with a silver stream curving through the valley. It was one that Antonia had painted one day when she was near the excavation site, then finished in the studio.

"The light here is better," Vittorio observed. "More luminous."

After some deliberation and some most adverse comments on two pictures she had done in Florence, Vittorio offered to buy the one of Pisa and that of the Perugian plain.

Antonia left him to decide the sum he would pay, for Robert was also here and she knew he would not allow her to be cheated in any way.

"Now you will proceed to work much harder and paint well," encouraged Vittorio, as he prepared to leave. "I will take my two with me and if I should sell them to rich Americans, I will also perhaps offer you more money for your future work."

Antonia thanked him, and now he also complimented her on her spoken Italian. "You are most industrious," he told her.

Robert accompanied Vittorio to the ground floor while Antonia began to repack her paintings, slipping cardboard corner pieces over the frame edges to protect them.

When Robert returned she wheeled around quickly.

"Oh, Robert!" she exclaimed, dancing with delight. "Two pictures sold! I owe it all to you." She put her hands on his shoulders and impulsively kissed him on the cheek.

Robert clasped her around the waist, lifted her in the air and swung her in a circle.

Then she saw Talbot standing in the open doorway of the room.

"I'm sorry. I seem to have intruded on some celebration," he said acidly.

Robert looked startled. "Talbot!" he called as he went to the door. "Antonia has sold—"

But Talbot Drury had already disappeared along the corridor.

CHAPTER NINE

THE Lido at Ponte San Giovanni was a pleasant place in which to spend a hot afternoon, but some of the pleasure had been extinguished for Antonia by Talbot's abrupt departure this morning when he had apparently witnessed that ridiculous little piece of byplay with Robert.

Did he believe that on the pretext of a picture exhibition in an untenanted room in the hotel she had nothing better to do than flirt with Robert?

Yet the incident perturbed her, for she realised that subconsciously she desired Talbot's good opinion of her.

When she and Robert had enjoyed their fill of alternate swimming and sunbathing, they went to the Volumni to see the beautiful urns surmounted by carved effigies of the dead, but also many scenes of Etruscan life.

"Did you go to Volterra when you were in Florence?" asked Robert, as they gazed at the beautiful winged women supporting a large urn with a reclining statue on top.

"Yes, Philip and I visited it on our way back from Pisa, but it happened to be a day when he wasn't very well and I thought it would tire him too much to go to the Etruscan museum there, although we saw the ramparts which must have been awe-inspiring at one time to the town's enemies."

"I haven't been there," Robert admitted. "In fact I'll confess that apart from the large towns like Florence and Pisa and, of course, some of those in the south, Rome, Naples, Sorrento, I haven't seen much of Italy. I could claim, I suppose, that I haven't had time."

"It would take a lifetime to travel about Italy and see even a tenth of the treasures that are here. One fascinating sight we did see in Volterra was a whole street with workshops all for carving alabaster. Workmen sat at benches carving the stone—it looked fairly easy, so I assume it was soft—and they were making all kinds of bowls and ornaments, ash-trays and so on. Some specialised in fish and birds and little animals."

"Talbot should take you there some time," said Robert. "If he wants you to be interested in the work he's doing, he ought to take a little time off now and again to encourage you."

Antonia smiled. She thought it very unlikely that Talbot would offer her a day's outing to Volterra or anywhere else.

When she and Robert left the Museum at closing time they went to a nearby café in the main piazza and Robert ordered glasses of wine.

Antonia was idly watching the people, couples ambling along at a snail's pace, family parties with daintily-dressed children and several indulgent aunts and uncles, when her attention was caught by Robert's shout of "Talbot!"

Talbot had actually passed the café and now turned, hesitated and then only reluctantly, it seemed, retraced his few steps and stood looming over Antonia and Robert.

"Sit down and join us in a drink of something," invited Robert.

Talbot agreed, but after some time Antonia came to the conclusion that Robert's friendly gesture had been a mistake, for Talbot spread an aura of gloom. Each topic of conversation died for want of animation and, for her part, Antonia was glad when Talbot rose to go.

"I'm going down to Florence later in the week," Robert said unexpectedly. "I thought I'd take a few days off to see Cleo, although the hotel manager is not exactly thrilled about it just as our busy season is beginning."

For the first time since Talbot had sat with them he smiled. "Give Cleo and her mother my best regards," he said, then walked away across the piazza.

"What's biting him?" muttered Robert when Talbot was well out of earshot. "You must have put a damper on him somehow, Tonia."

"Not my fault. I take no responsibility at all for any of his moods. Put it down to the work he does, all among excavations and tombs and statuary."

Robert shook his head slowly. "I don't know how he can give his entire energies, his mind, his heart, to digging up the past, and such a remote past at that!"

"He might just as easily be puzzled by your insistence on hotel management and think that's a footling sort of occupation." After a pause she added, "I'm glad you're going to Florence, Cleo will be delighted."

"That isn't what you said a week or two ago. You told me to let Cleo have her fling."

"Well, there are times to be with her and times to stay away," was Antonia's rather lame reply. She was aware that she had contradictated her earlier advice, but that was before the Italian count had appeared on the scene.

"I'm never sure of my welcome with Cleo," continued Robert, speaking his thoughts aloud. "I often feel that I've arrived at a very inconvenient moment just when she's making the grade with some new conquest."

"Surely that's the exact moment to arrive," she assured him.

Robert was more perceptive than Antonia had credited and all might yet go well when he was patient enough to wait for her to recover from these heady flights into romantic adventures.

Antonia hoped that no word of the rumoured Italian "count" had come to Robert's ears. Yet even if it had or he discovered this new attachment, might it not give Robert the chance of cutting the nobleman down to size?

Spurred by her success in selling two pictures, Antonia worked hard for the next day or two in the studio until the evening when Philip was due to arrive back in Perugia.

After she had returned to the hotel and dressed for dinner, she went down to the courtyard bar to join Philip and was surprised to see him engaged in an apparently stimulating conversation with Talbot. The two men, with glasses of vermouth in their hands, were laughing their heads off, but as Antonia approached, they composed themselves, ordered her aperitif and sat down at a nearby table.

She asked Philip a few questions about his trip and he launched into an amusing anecdote about an incident in Naples.

"I was just telling Talbot here about it," he explained, but Antonia doubted whether that had really been the subject of such merriment between them.

It was natural that Talbot should dine with Philip and Antonia, but the two men did most of the talking. She hoped fervently that Philip would not try to devise some method of leaving her alone with Talbot for the rest of the evening.

Actually, Philip was not to blame, for it was Talbot who suggested that he and Antonia might like to visit the store-room and see his latest find.

Philip expressed his admiration of the ingenuity that went to the fashioning of a plaque or bowl from an assortment of jagged pieces.

"You haven't seen this yet, Antonia," Talbot pointed to part of a necklace in the process of being cleaned.

"Gold?" she queried, examining the three ornamented semi-circles attached to a curved rod.

"Yes. We can only do the rough cleaning. The museum here in Perugia will finish it and add it to their collection."

In Talbot's voice was all the pride of discovery and nothing of possessive envy. Other people such as Robert and certainly Cleo could never comprehend why Talbot would want to spend his life in this kind of work, but Antonia understood. He was like a mountain climber who climbs only for the reason that the "mountains are there."

"How is the tunnel progressing under Luciano's house?" she asked.

"Slowly, but we can't expect a mad rush," Talbot answered. "Why don't you come and look at it tomorrow? You could even make some sketches if we can get enough light down there, and I think we can."

She hesitated. Philip had only just returned from his business trip and she owed him at least this first day if he wanted her to accompany him on an excursion somewhere.

She looked around the store-room to ask him, but he had quietly disappeared.

"I'll ask Philip, but I shall probably be going out with him."

"Just as you like," murmured Talbot casually as he replaced the fragments of necklace.

There was nothing more to say. She moved to the store-room door and called "Goodnight" to him.

He looked up quickly. "Yes, of course, it's pleasant for you to have Philip here. I expect you miss Robert."

His back was to the light and his face in shadow. She stared at him for a few seconds, bit back the retort that she might not miss Robert half as much as Talbot missed Cleo, then closed the door behind her.

When she found Philip again and told him of Talbot's suggestion for next day, he said, "Oh, I'm not thrilled at the idea. You go by all means, if he wants you to work there, but I'd rather stay here and catch up with my correspondence. I've a pile of notes that I made on my meetings in Rome and elsewhere. I shall forget what we all said if I don't work on them immediately while events are fresh in my mind."

But after Talbot's oblique thrust about missing Robert's company, Antonia decided next morning to work in her studio on a picture she had nearly finished.

Francesca rose about midday as usual, yawned her way around the studio, drank several cups of black coffee which Antonia made, then started work on some plates.

Antonia admired Francesca's skill and steady hand as the designs took shape. "These are copies of the famous Deruta pottery," she explained, "but here in Perugia we also have our own traditional patterns."

About five o'clock Antonia concluded that she had done all she could to the current picture. "If I tinker any more with it, I shall only irritate myself. I'd better leave it."

"That is best," agreed Francesca. "Look at it in a week's time and you will find the faults."

Antonia knew from experience that what satisfied one's eye today became with the passage of even a short time merely a display of assembled errors.

She cleaned her brushes, scraped her palette and put away the canvas among the others stacked against the wall.

It was too early to return to the Margharita and possibly disturb Philip, and it occurred to her to take the bus up to Luciano Pontelli's temporary house in the village not far from the excavation site.

The house was only a comparatively short walk down from the main road, and after a day in Francesca's stuffy studio, Antonia enjoyed the exercise now in the early evening when a cool breeze tempered the day's heat.

The two small children were playing outside the house and ran towards her when she approached the open door. Emilia shouted a welcome and Signora Pontelli interrupted her preparation of the evening meal to offer Antonia a glass of wine and a small cake.

With excited gestures Emilia and her mother pointed out how they had made what to Antonia was a pitiful shack into something resembling a home. The walls were freshly whitewashed, the stone floor scrubbed and laid with straw matting. Curtains on a long pole divided what was evidently the sleeping accommodation from the living space. Clearly, the Pontelli family were delighted with their new residence, even though from the outside it appeared nothing but a tumbledown stone hut.

Antonia was pleased with her ability to converse with the Pontellis in Italian, but she found that they overestimated her capacity to understand their rapid comments and questions.

"*Adagio*," she kept saying to them, although that word with its musical connotation always made her giggle, especially when she had first seen it in Florence at the entrance to a garage as an injunction to drivers.

The two young children ran in shouting that Martina was coming. Antonia allowed herself to be almost dragged outside and she watched Martina walking down the road, balancing a huge pitcher on her head. Of course, there would be no water laid on and no doubt the girls had to make many daily journeys to the nearest well.

Almost at once, an open truck with a dozen or so men sitting in it approached from the opposite direction and waved and shouted to the Pontelli girls as Martina's young man friend, Guido, alighted. They greeted Antonia, too, when they recognised her and, to her surprise, Stefano also clambered out of the lorry, which resumed its dust-raising journey to Perugia.

"This is a very pleasant idea you have," said Stefano to Antonia. "Do you come here many times to the Pontellis?"

"No. This is the first time. I felt sorry that Luciano had been given such a poor little house, so small and poky for a family of that size."

He gave her his charming smile. "In summer, one can live outdoors much of the time."

"Yes, but the winter? Will Luciano have a better house by then?"

Stefano shrugged, and it was obvious that he regarded whatever kind of home the Pontellis obtained as no real concern of his.

Emilia brought out more wine and a large piece of clean sacking and a couple of cushions so that the visitors could sit on the ground without soiling their clothes. The courtesy was scarcely necessary, for the men were in their working clothes and Antonia wore a cotton dress.

There was a great deal of laughter and lively chatter until Luciano returned from work. Although his greetings were polite, he frowned at his two sisters and demanded in an undertone to know why they were not indoors assisting their mother with the evening meal. The pair of them scuttled off indoors, completely obedient to Luciano's orders.

Stefano called to the boy, "How is your camera working?"

Luciano nodded. "Very well."

"Bring it out and take photographs of us and the Signorina Antonia," Stefano suggested.

The boy moved wearily to the hut.

"Stefano, he's tired after a long day's work," protested Antonia. "He doesn't want to be bothered taking snaps of us."

"We are also tired," said Martina's friend, Guido. "Now we are glad to rest for a while."

Luciano emerged from the little house followed by his entire family. Even the mother spared a few moments from her cooking.

Luciano took several shots, Stefano took one that included the boy surrounded by his relatives, then there had to be pictures of Martina and Guido and a group with Antonia between him and Stefano.

Luciano announced that the film was finished and Stefano offered to take it with him and develop and print the snaps for the boy.

Antonia declared that she must be going home soon, although the Pontellis invited her to share supper with them.

"Then if you will not stay, we will show you a local dance," said Martina.

The two girls with Guido and Stefano began a lively dance accompanied by their own singing with Luciano clapping his hands.

Antonia watched, envying the lithe grace of the two

164

girls who could dance barefoot on a rough, stony piece of dusty ground.

"Come and join us. It is simple!" cried Stefano.

Antonia accepted the invitation and Emilia stepped out of the group, but demonstrated the movements so that Antonia could follow.

The dance was a vigorous one and Antonia wondered how the Italians had enough breath for dancing and singing and laughing all the same time.

She stumbled on a large boulder and Stefano caught her in his arms to save her from falling. True, he seemed reluctant to release her, but she gently disentangled herself from his clasp and they resumed the dance. A moment later she noticed that a car had stopped outside the house only a few yards away from the patch of earth. The dancers stopped singing.

Talbot stuck his head out of the car window. "Are you staying up here, Antonia? Or do you want a lift down to Perugia?"

She would have been glad to refuse, but she was not at all sure if there would be any other transport and she could not expect Stefano to make some special arrangement for her if the last bus had already gone.

"Yes, thank you. I'll come in a moment," she replied after a few seconds' hesitation. She hastened indoors to the house to bid hasty goodbyes and promise to come again soon.

When she reached the car, Stefano was standing beside it.

"D'you want a lift, too?" Talbot asked his assistant.

The man shook his head very decisively. "No, I shall come back later. I have friends with Vespas."

Antonia would have been glad, for once, of his company, for she knew that the moment Talbot was driving along the road he would probably read her a lecture about the folly of becoming too friendly with the Pontellis and especially with Stefano and the other men working on the site.

She was slightly surprised when he started off on quite a different tack.

"I thought you couldn't spare time for the site today?" he said.

"I don't think I gave you that impression," she returned. "I told you that I might have to go out with Philip."

"But you changed your mind."

"No, he did. He had work to do in the hotel. I've spent most of the day in the studio."

"And then you went to the Pontellis'. Why?"

"I don't really think it's any of your business, but I'll tell you. I wanted to see what that poor little hut was like and whether they were reasonably comfortable there."

"And were you satisfied that they'd not been dumped into a cowshed?" he queried.

"For the time being, yes. But I hope that your promise of a better house is going to be fulfilled."

"Not my promise. The local authorities'," he snapped.

"I see. So you've washed your hands of Luciano and his family affairs now that you've got what you wanted from his other old shack."

"I don't understand why you're so vitally concerned over their accommodation."

"Perhaps I'm not quite so immersed in ancient civilisations that I have no thought for human problems in the present time."

"The Pontellis should be well satisfied that they have such a stout champion on their side."

His tone was so sarcastic that she could not bring herself to answer without breaking into a stormy quarrel. He drove a mile or two before he spoke again. "You must try not to let your friendship with the Pontellis involve you too much with Stefano. He's an excellent assistant, but he has a roving eye and considers himself quite a Lothario."

"A Casanova, too?" she queried icily. "I don't think you need concern yourself about my friendships."

"But it does concern me," he retorted. "I'm responsible for introducing you to Stefano, to Luciano, and the rest of his family."

"And you believe you must protect me from all harm?"

"Oh, Antonia, be realistic, for goodness' sake!" he said angrily, swerving to avoid a cyclist.

"Let's not discuss the matter any more," she said quietly. "I don't really enjoy driving with an angry motorist."

He gave her a dagger-sharp glance, then fixed his attention on the road.

They covered the rest of the short journey in complete silence and Antonia reflected that she could easily have avoided this stormy scene if she had remembered that Talbot would undoubtedly have to pass the Pontellis' house on his way home. Either she ought to have left earlier or been inside the house when he would never have known that she had been there.

At dinner with Philip she let the two men do most of the conversation, merely putting in a word now and again so that Philip would not remark upon her silence.

But when they had finished and were taking their coffee in the courtyard, Philip suggested brightly, "Why don't you two go off somewhere for the evening? I'm told that there are summer concerts in the open air."

Antonia slowly moved her head to glance at Talbot, who studiously averted his face. "I think Talbot has work to do in his store-room," she said in the kindest tone she could manage, "and I thought I might go down to one of the cafés and talk to my Scandinavian friends."

She excused herself and went out of the hotel. She had to make a show of walking down the Corso Vannucci whether she wanted to or not. At the beautiful Priors' Palace and the great fountain which she had sketched so many times from different aspects she turned away from the cafés and walked towards the Etruscan Gate, a spot which always had a calming influence on her. Perugia's stirring history when passions had been so violent and bloodshed so inordinate that the cathedral steps had to be washed with wine and reconsecrated, was apt to be overpowering if you were aware of atmosphere in old buildings that whispered their secrets as you passed.

A wisp of annoyance crossed her mind when she found that the stone bench near the foot of the Gate was occupied by a solitary man. Well, it would not have been wise for her to sit there alone in the dark, even though the Gate was floodlit.

She passed the seat, intending to mount the long, twisting flight of steps, when a voice called "Tonia!" When she turned sharply she was face to face with Talbot.

"Were you going to walk right by me?" he asked.

"I didn't see it was you," she admitted, then added, "Surely you wouldn't encourage me to stare at every man I happen to see sitting alone on a bench?"

"No. But you could have glanced my way after I'd taken the trouble to come down here in search of you."

He had guided her imperceptibly towards the stone seat.

"How did you know I'd be here?" she asked.

"Easy. I remembered that your Scandinavian friends, Ingrid and Sven, had left Perugia weeks ago."

A queer exultant thrill sharpened her perception. So he had been interested enough to follow her, then take the short cut down the steps. Was it merely because he thought it his duty to protect an English girl in a foreign city? She hoped that inclination was stronger than his sense of duty.

Then he spoke, and her warm feeling of contentment in his company melted away on the cool night air.

"Why do we fight each other?" he asked.

She shrugged. "I suppose we're not on the same wavelength. We're just two people who rub each other up the wrong way."

"You didn't think that when you first knew me."

"No, perhaps not," she agreed. "But since then

you've taken plenty of opportunity to treat me like a naughty child."

"And how many opportunities have you snatched to snub me and show me very plainly that I'm in the way?"

"In the way of what? Or whom?" she demanded, a spurt of anger creeping into her tone.

"I don't know. I find it all very .puzzling. I can't make out whether you've become fond of Robert or—"

"Why would Robert come into it? He's mad about Cleo."

"He might have changed his mind, I suppose?" Talbot said thoughtfully.

"As you hope that Cleo has changed hers?" she queried.

"Why should I hope that?"

"Well, you've done everything you could to come between Cleo and Robert," she accused him. "I know she's young and rather flighty, but you might have had more consideration for Robert."

"What on earth are you saying, Tonia?"

She hesitated, but she had now committed herself to this headlong path of indictment. She longed to hear his denials.

"As soon as she and her mother went to Florence, you had to go galloping after them."

"You must be crazy to suggest that! You know, more than anyone else, why I went there."

"I know your excuse was the museums and you wanted to check on exhibits to trace the fakes. It was all very plausible."

"Plausible! Is that what you think when the only real reason why I went there was because—" He broke off abruptly.

"Because what?" she prompted softly. His nearness and his resentful disclaimers had for a few magic moments encouraged her to believe that he might just possibly have followed her, not Cleo, to Florence.

"Oh, what's the use of trying to explain anything to

you?" he burst out angrily as he rose. "Come on, it's late. I'd better take you back to the hotel."

"I'm sorry if I seemed to entangle you with Cleo and her affairs," she said in a small, humble voice.

He made no answer and as they climbed the steps she was reminded of that other occasion, a happier one, when he had met her at the Etruscan Gate and they had ascended these flights of steps between the dark, silent houses.

Antonia vowed that while she remained in Perugia she would never come again to the Gate if she could avoid it. The ancient, towering archway held the wrong memories for her now. She deluded herself that she had glimpsed into a future unimaginably inviting, even rapturous, but now she knew that she had succeeded in alienating Talbot completely and conclusively.

CHAPTER TEN

WHEN Philip announced his intention of leaving for home Antonia realised that this was also her cue for departure from Perugia. There was no reason to stay, except that she was still trying to obtain a better house for Luciano and would have liked to know if all her efforts had been fruitless.

"You must write and tell me about it, Robert," she said one evening in the Margharita. "I'm sure he moved into that hut only on the strength of Talbot's promises of something better."

"I'll do what I can," he promised. "I'm sorry you're leaving, but I understand that you can't spend all your exciting year's travel in one place."

"I've stayed overlong in Perugia," she murmured, reflecting on how little the words conveyed, for her whole world had been shattered, remade and destroyed again by an idiotic belief that she had fallen in love with Talbot. No ceramics expert could ever have succeeded in piecing together the fragments of happy contentment when so much had been torn apart by distrust and bitterness.

She spoke about her pictures. "I don't really think I can clutter myself with all those unsaleable efforts I've done here. Where d'you suggest I should leave them?"

Robert was thoughtful for a moment or two. "Well, Francesca will need the space as she'll probably want to let half the studio. We have store-rooms here, but they're rather full at the moment. Why don't you store them for the time being in the one that Talbot rents for his discoveries?"

"Yes, I suppose so." She was not too happy about asking favours from him, but no doubt Robert would settle the matter for her.

Mrs. Norwood and Cleo had returned with Robert, who now seemed in much better spirits. When Antonia found the chance to ask Cleo how matters had prospered with the Italian count, Cleo giggled.

"You are a soft one, Antonia!" she exclaimed delightedly. "As if it would last! We both knew that, his highness and I. The purpose of the exercise was to spread a little uncertainty in all directions."

"And did the exercise succeed?" queried Antonia, laughing.

"Oh, yes. Perfectly. I'm determined not to fall into Robert's lap like a little ripe plum."

"Why not? He has everything, looks, charm, talent, immense wealth—and, more than that, he loves you to distraction."

Cleo rubbed the tip of her finger against the side of her dainty nose. "So he does, but there's not much fun in knowing that he's there whenever you want him. I expect to have a bit of excitement, something to chase, before I walk up the aisle with anyone. A real hard nut to crack is what I like."

"Is that why you practised on Talbot?"

"Ah, Talbot!" murmured Cleo reflectively. "He's rather too much of a Dreary Drury for me. He never seems to be living in the present somehow, always comparing the charms of statues in the museums with what he might find in his excavations. You'd better take him on, Antonia. He's more in your line."

Antonia smiled. "Oh, you've changed your mind considerably since the time you warned me off first Robert, then Talbot."

"Oh, I've never regarded you as a serious rival—"

"Thanks very much for the compliment!" Antonia could not restrain her laughter.

"I didn't mean it that way," protested Cleo. "All right. I did. But you know, Antonia, if you went the right way about it, you could hook the men in no time."

"I must have lessons from you," said Antonia. "But since you're so smug, how d'you know I haven't been hooking the men, as you so succinctly put it, right and left while you've been away? Robert, for instance, ready to be twined round my little finger."

"Robert will do so much for you and sings your praises so constantly that I know that you're both just good friends," Cleo stated with the authority of one who has worked out the logic of all human relations.

On the day that Philip was leaving, Antonia accompanied him to the airport at Pisa. She gave him last-minute messages for her mother. "I'll write to her every week as usual," she promised, "and as soon as I have an address in Naples or elsewhere I'll let you both know."

"Funny thing, I thought you'd stay a long time in Perugia," he said.

"I have stayed a long time," she told him emphatically. "I ought to see the rest of Italy while I have the chance, even though I've been on visits to some of the other towns."

"Yes, of course. Good painting!"

"I shall do my best work. I've been lucky to sell the odd one or two, mainly through Robert's good efforts."

"Robert," murmured Philip ruminatively. "He's wasted on that little fluffy-head Cleo. I should have thought that you and he would have had a lot more in common."

She laughed. "It isn't always couples who have a lot in common who marry each other. The wildest extremes meet."

He nodded. "You're right, and what extremes! You wonder—"

"—what on earth he saw in her!" Antonia finished for him.

They both laughed, but she knew that these were the moments when Philip particularly missed his wife, Marion, who had died about ten years ago just when his business affairs had soared to a peak of success. Many times he had confided to Antonia that it would have been his delight to give pleasure to Marion on his trips abroad to distant places where they had both longed to go.

When Antonia arrived back in Perugia, she ran full tilt into Talbot standing inside the hotel vestibule.

"Robert tells me you have a lot of paintings to store somewhere," he said, almost without preamble.

"Yes. Have you space in your store-room?" She preferred to tackle the situation in the most direct way.

"Of course. Perhaps I could help you to bring them here tonight after dinner?" he suggested.

"Thank you. That would be fine."

She escaped as quickly as possible to her room and changed for dinner. She had no choice but to accept his offer, although she would have preferred to collect the paintings and hand them over to Robert as go-between.

Almost for the first time she blessed the presence of Cleo and Mrs. Norwood at the dinner table shared with Talbot. Alone with him she would have found nothing to say and there would have been the most awkward pauses.

At the end of the meal he excused himself and Antonia to Mrs. Norwood and Cleo. "Tonia and I have a job of work to do collecting her pictures from the studio."

Cleo gave Antonia a grin that expressed a world of innuendo. "See you tomorrow. 'Bye—*Tonia*."

But the studio visit proved to be a very business-like matter. Talbot carried the paintings down the several flights of stairs and stowed them in the waiting taxi. Antonia picked up her battered tin box of colours, her bundle of brushes, the palette knives, while Talbot took the easel down.

She took a last glance around the studio where she had spent happy working hours in the company of Francesca, shut the door and locked it. This was the end of a chapter in every sense and she wondered if she would ever again paint the Umbrian scene, the hill-top landscape or those enchanting little corners of Perugia, all contrasting highlights and shadows.

Talbot stood outside on the pavement. "There's just about room for you to squeeze in the taxi, I think, but I'll walk."

Antonia clambered in, narrowly missing putting her foot through a finished canvas, and sat on the only few inches of space remaining. Oh, it was true, there was no room for Talbot unless he sat on the roof, but she realised how strong was her unconscious longing for the sweet intimacy of a shared and crowded taxi.

To her surprise he was alighting from another taxi outside the Margharita as Antonia and her cargo arrived.

"I came quickly," Talbot explained, "because I realised you might need help in unloading."

"Thank you. That was very thoughtful of you," she said, and she meant it sincerely, but the upward glance he gave her implied that he thought she was being scornful. Why must he always take everything in the worst possible way? she thought irritably.

In the store-room as Talbot stacked the pictures against the walls, Antonia made what she considered was to be her last gesture of friendliness towards this man who had succeeded so well in unsettling her.

"I wondered if there was any—a particular picture that you might like to have," she said tentatively. "You can't choose now in artificial light, but in daylight you're welcome to one—if you want it."

He came towards her. "Of course I'd like to have one. There's a small one of the Etruscan Gate, if you don't mind parting with that."

Oh, take the Etruscan Gate, she thought. I don't want to be reminded of it. Aloud she said, "Yes, of course. Choose whichever you like."

"I've also something to give you, Tonia," he said quietly. From his pocket he took out an envelope and placed it in her hands. "It's a small cheque in payment —or part payment, that is—for all the marvellous work you've done at the site. I'm sorry you're going just now when we're getting down to what I'm convinced is a very exciting discovery—but—" He broke off and shrugged. "I apologise for not giving you a cheque or two already, but I had the impression that your money matters were satisfactory for the time being."

"Thank you," she whispered, near to tears, her throat aching.

"And something else." He turned away and brought out a large, gaily-wrapped parcel. "Not even in Naples will you get Perugina chocolates."

"Thank you again," she murmured, as she took the box from his hands.

"Tonia!" he said sharply. "Why are you crying?"

"I—I don't know."

He put his hands on her elbows and stared at her downbent face.

Then the door opened and Robert came in.

"I've had your easel brought down here, Antonia," he said breezily. "It was left in the service lift."

"Oh—er—thank you, Robert," she managed to say.

He looked across at Talbot, who stood with his hands in his pockets.

"Everything packed in?" asked Robert.

"Yes, everything," answered Talbot shortly.

Antonia saw her chance of escape and took it, stopping only to call goodnight to both men.

In her room in seclusion she dabbed at her eyes, repowdered her face, but to no avail, for slow tears rolled down her cheeks at the thought of all that she was leaving behind in Perugia. If only Robert had not barged in at that moment—!

Two days before Antonia was due to leave, Robert arranged a small farewell party for her at the Margharita. Besides Cleo and Mrs. Norwood, all the friends she had made in Perugia were there, except those from the Italian class who had now left. Everyone except Talbot, who was so busy working on the site that he had not returned to the hotel for four days. Antonia told herself that of course he had not known about the party, but she was not really comforted by that view. Even if he'd known, he might still have stayed away. She had not seen him since the evening in the storeroom and might never see him again.

At midday next day, Robert gave her the exciting news that Talbot had struck the discovery he'd been working for all these weeks.

"A new hypogeum!" exclaimed Robert. "The press and the museum officials are all up there, waiting to see what's inside."

"Oh, marvellous!" At last she had the perfect excuse for visiting the excavation site and congratulating Talbot even as she said goodbye. "When will it be possible to see it?"

"Not for a day or two at least. Possibly longer," said Robert. "The last thing he wants is people tramping about before he's ready for them."

"I shan't tramp about anywhere," she retorted. "I know better than that. I'd just like to see Talbot's success, that's all. Luciano's, too. He'll have a plaque fixed there to say it was once his home."

Antonia was impatient to set off by taxi or any vehicle that would get her to the site, but Cleo said, "Let's have lunch first. Then you can come in my car. If it's all prohibited to the public, we'll say we're the best friends of the explorer himself. That ought to let us in."

Antonia made the best pretence of eating that she could and she and Cleo drove off immediately after the meal, much to Mrs. Norwood's displeasure.

"You shouldn't be driving in the hot afternoon, Cleo," she scolded.

The excavation site was swarming with people and Cleo had to park her car some distance from the usual place.

Part of Luciano's old house had been dismantled, but the rest remained, although it now appeared only precariously supported.

Antonia and Cleo approached the group clustered about the entrance to the tunnel, but were not allowed to go any nearer.

"Tell someone that we're Talbot's artistic assistants," urged Cleo. "You speak Italian better than I."

Antonia found Signor Lombardi, the official from the museum, to whom Talbot had introduced her some time ago.

He shook his head at her request. "Perhaps you would wait for Signor Drury's permission?"

"Of course, but will you let him know that we are here? Our names are Antonia and Cleo.

He smiled his promise to do so.

Cleo was talking to Stefano when Antonia rejoined her.

"Later, they say, when Talbot says the word," she reported.

Stefano rummaged in his jacket pocket and brought out a wallet of snaps. "Luciano's house. Remember?" he said.

"Yes. Those he took when I called there," muttered Antonia, remembering Talbot's angry attitude when he found her there and drove her home in his car.

"See? Guido, Martina, you, Emilia, me?" pointed out Stefano eagerly.

Cleo examined each one as it was passed to her. "M'm," she murmured, then whistled softly. "I'd no idea that your circle extended so far, Tonia. You'd better not let Talbot see these. Oh, here's one of you and Stefano alone. Hide that!"

Stefano grinned. "Not possible. Luciano showed all to the boss."

"And what did the boss say?" queried Cleo.

Stefano shrugged. "He was not pleased to see the Signorina Antonia among us as though it could be a party."

Antonia decided to make the best of a bad job. She laughed lightly. "Talbot really knew all about it. He passed the house when we were all madly dancing."

She returned the snaps to Stefano. It was ironic that she had been so anxious to give Luciano a camera and, like a boomerang, his snapshots had contrived to put her in an entirely false position.

Someone near the tunnel was waving and Antonia ran to join the crowd of reporters and photographers.

Talbot emerged, his face dirty with a stubble of beard, his fair hair dark with soil. He looked almost too weary to stand, but when his gaze fell on Antonia, he gave her a half-smile and beckoned to her.

"I heard about your discovery," she explained. "I had to come."

He gave her a slightly twisted grin. "I could have done with your help in some of the earlier stages, when the photographs were not enough, but we're near the end now."

His tone was like the flick of a whip and she turned away to control her trembling mouth.

Other men crowded around him, asking questions, until he waved them away, promising further information the moment it could be given.

Then, to her astonishment, he wheeled round on her. "Grab a tin hat and follow us if you want to see anything."

She was handed a helmet by one of the workmen and although it fell over her ears when she tightened the chin strap, it was at least some protection. She had come clad in dark stretch-pants and a cotton shirt in the hope that she might be allowed to enter the tunnel.

A few electric lights had been rigged up inside the cellar of Luciano's house from a small generator. The tunnel went only a short distance before there was a sharp descent.

"This is where there was once a flight of steps," called Talbot. He was leading the party and his voice echoed and boomed in what seemed to be a cavern.

Antonia experienced a tremor of fear at the thought of the massive weight of the hillside above their heads, thousands of tons of solid rock. The steep pitch flattened out and she had to take small crouching steps to avoid hitting her steel-helmeted head on the uneven roof. One of the workmen following her shone a torch to help her miss the worst bumps in the floor.

A gust of air came from a side opening and she was tremendously relieved, for down here the air was stifling and she realised she was gasping aloud.

Then along a narrower tunnel where she had to crawl sideways and edge round jutting rocks. At last, when her head was swimming and she longed to lie down and relax, she heard Talbot's booming voice announce that he had reached the opening of the hypogeum itself.

The press photographer took his pictures as best he could in the confined space, a smaller and nimbler official from the museum than Signor Lombardi, who was too portly to wriggle through these underground labyrinths, surveyed the opening first, made a few notes, asked Talbot questions.

Antonia leaned against the side of the tunnel, awed by the thought that perhaps she was about to see a small room that had lain buried for two and a half thousand years.

The opening to the chamber had been blocked with a bronze grille, which had already been cut from the doorway sides and taken away to be carefully cleaned before replacing it.

Now Talbot and his handful of followers stood upright in the hollowed secret resting-place of some eminent nobleman, possibly Etruscan, who had lived three or four centuries B.C.

In the gloom of torches, there was perhaps little to see yet, for more than two thousand years of dust had to be gently removed to reveal the treasures. The dead nobleman's ashes had been encased in a marble casket, surmounted by a reclining statue of himself, but in no passive attitude. The figure, even only partially cleaned, was full of vitality, showing the man raised on one elbow and with his other outstretched hand taking a goblet from an unseen attendant.

"Wonderful! Marvellous!" exclaimed the museum official. "You will be famous, Signor Drury, for your discovery."

"A great deal of work remains to be done," returned Talbot.

The photographer took pictures, but Talbot informed him that his own assistant, Stefano, could provide better exposures.

"He can give you some prints for the press when the museum authorities release them," Talbot told him.

Antonia saw now that her sketching ability would have been of some help to Talbot, in conjunction with the photographs. The walls of the room were carved to imitate the wooden beams and other interior features of Etruscan houses. Careful brushing and scraping would reveal a wealth of detail about the daily life of the Etruscans.

She regretted that she had not brought her sketch-block with her, but there was nothing she could do about that now.

The party retraced their way along the subterranean passages and emerged into the dazzling sunlight of late afternoon.

Antonia was aware that if so many other faces were dirty and dust-streaked, so was her own, and she walked towards Cleo's car, intending to find tissues to wipe away the marks of a tunnel journey.

Suddenly there was shouting and a commotion as a car moved slowly forward and toppled over a section of the site where a fairly large square had been mathematically dug out. Men ran to the spot and Talbot broke away from the group to whom he had been talking.

Antonia heard his hoarse shout of "Cleo! Cleo!" as he ran past her towards the car. She hurried behind him. She realised that Cleo might have been sitting in the car, but while these thoughts entered the upper layers of her mind, her deeper warnings whispered that Talbot's concern when Cleo might be in danger was unmistakable evidence that she still meant a great deal to him.

At the foot of the cut earth, men strained and heaved to lift the car, which was apparently empty, while Talbot directed them to keep the car from damaging the side walls of the excavation.

Cleo appeared, smiling, unhurt, and glanced ruefully at her car now being lifted with ropes.

"What happened?" she asked.

Talbot turned savagely towards her. "Couldn't you take more care where you park?" he rapped out.

"It wasn't my fault. I wasn't even there. How could I know that someone was going to push it over?"

Antonia turned away. It was a common enough reaction, to scold the person who'd given you a fright, like a mother who recovers her lost child and smacks him for disappearing.

She was in earshot just long enough to hear Talbot say in a calmer voice, "Well, at any rate, you're safe. You might have been badly injured."

She walked back to the remains of Luciano's old house and found Stefano. In the tunnel an idea had occurred to her and now she explained it to him.

"Ah Signorina Antonia, I do not think it possible," he demurred.

"Why not? You've been there several times. All I need is light. You're the best person to provide this carefully so that nothing important is damaged or destroyed."

He still shook his head. "The Signor Drury is the best person. He will not like it if I go with you there."

"Stefano! What are you afraid of? Ghosts?"

"No, but the *signor* will be displeased."

"Not perhaps if I can do some sketches of the secret room. He said earlier today that I could have helped him if I'd been here. All I need is a couple of hours tonight. Down there the daylight makes no difference. After tonight it will be too late. Tomorrow I leave for Naples."

Reluctantly, he agreed to meet her at the Pontellis' at nine o'clock and escort her along the tunnel.

She rejoined Cleo, sympathising with the girl about the damaged car.

"I don't know how it went over that cliff!" Cleo protested loudly. "I'm positive the brakes were on. Someone must have shifted it out of their way."

"Is it possible to drive it home?" Antonia asked.

"Not really, but I've fixed up that we can go back to Perugia in someone else's car."

The two girls transferred all their belongings to the other man's car. Antonia was impatient to return and, for once, Cleo was not anxious to dally.

"I thought you might want to stay there longer and come back with Talbot," she said to Antonia.

"Don't push me at the man," Antonia replied lightly.

Cleo gave her an amused smile. "I think you're learning. That's right. Let him look around for you and find you're not there."

Back at the hotel Antonia unpacked her sketch-block, pencils and other tools, changed into another pair of stretch-pants, a clean shirt and thin jacket. Stefano had promised to borrow a boiler-suit for her and he would have helmets for them both.

"I am very careful about knocking my head," he had said, roaring with laughter. "It is all I have."

Her absence at dinner would not be noticeable, she thought; in her immediate circle, everyone would conclude that she was with someone else.

She ate a quick meal at a snack bar in the town, then took a taxi to a spot a short distance from the Pontellis' house. When she paid him and told him not to wait, he gave her a knowing smile, evidently thinking that she had a secret assignation with a lover.

Stefano met her as arranged. "I have borrowed a friend's Vespa, so that I can take you back to Perugia." He had promised that he would find her some sort of transport for the return journey.

At the entrance to the tunnel, in what was the old cellar of Luciano's house, Stefano spoke to the guard. He had earlier warned Antonia that Signor Drury left a guard on duty all night.

Stefano showed the man his camera and torches, introduced Antonia as the necessary artist, then produced the boiler-suit and helmet.

Since the workman knew Stefano very well, there was no difficulty and he was obliging enough to switch on the generator, so that the first part of the tunnel was illuminated.

Traversing the dark passages was not easy, but Stefano was a helpful guide and eventually Antonia stood in the breathtaking chamber that had been fashioned in apparent likeness of a patrician house.

Stefano skilfully held torches and Antonia worked as quickly as she could, listening to the Italian's advice as to the pictures he had been able to take successfully, so that she could co-operate in sketching the points he had not been able to cover so well.

"The *signor* should be most grateful to us," he said. "We are doing good work for him."

Antonia, busily sketching, merely smiled. She was not looking for Talbot's gratitude, but this was perhaps the last gesture she could make to show him that at least she was proud of his success.

Stefano glanced at his watch. "It is late. We should be going now."

She was surprised to find that it was past midnight. As she and Stefano clambered back along the passage, she asked, "Does the *signor* think that robbers have been in the tomb at some time?"

"No, I think not. It is far inside the hill and perhaps Luciano's little house has been a safeguard."

"But there do not seem to be many objects or ornaments in there."

"They have already been taken to the museum," Stefano's voice came booming back at her. "Plates, most beautiful — and pots — and gold pins — and a griffin, carved—and—"

His voice was drowned by a shattering noise as though the whole hillside were caving in. Antonia crouched on her hands and knees, but although her head was protected, some piece of rock or wood hit her between the shoulder blades and almost knocked the breath out of her. Her torch had been wrenched from her grasp by the blow and she fumbled about for it in the dark. Rubble and dust continued to fall, choking her so that she gasped.

"Stefano!" she called, but knew her voice was little more than a whisper. "Stefano!" She could see nothing but pitch blackness around her.

She touched the tunnel walls with her hands, trying to find the direction of the passage. To her horror, she realised that she was hemmed in. The rock fall had blocked the tunnel completely in the direction which she thought was the exit. Behind her the passage was more than half blocked, but that led only back to the underground chamber.

"Stefano!" she called again and again. Now her voice was stronger and after what seemed an appalling time, she heard a thin echoing voice.

"Signorina Antonia!" came back the echo. "Where are you?"

"Down here," she shouted back. "I'm stuck!"

There was a long pause. Then Stefano's voice came again. "I must get help. Wait and be patient."

"Don't be too long!" she called. "There might be another collapse."

"Are you hurt?" he asked.

"No, I don't think so."

Then there was complete silence. Although she called every few minutes, there was no answer. Nothing but the tiny rustling movements of small stones and earth shifting and falling. She closed her eyes in fear. Supposing there was another fall? She would be completely trapped, even more than she was now. Supposing it took several days to dig the tunnel again, shore it up with supports, before rescuers could reach her?

What a piece of folly she had led Stefano into, merely to gratify her own wishes that she might be of service to Talbot. Well, she had done Talbot a fine service now, ruined his most successful work to date for the sake of a few sketches that might now be entirely worthless.

The sketches! In her first moments of fear she had dropped the case with the sketch-block. She began to scrabble on the uneven floor and luckily by accident found the torch which still worked. As she shone it on her tiny prison, her senses froze at the thought of the task which faced any possible rescuers. She realised that she must try to help herself, but first she must find the sketches.

The more she hunted about, searching the rock crevices, the more she lost her sense of direction. At last the torch shone on a corner of leather, but with dismay she saw that great boulders covered the rest of the case. Yet she must try to pull out the sketches from underneath. She worked at the case, tugging gently, easing it inch by inch, then resting while perspiration poured down her face. Gradually she was able to pull out the block without toppling the boulders over towards her.

She switched off the torch, for she might need its light for a long time yet. When she had rested for a while, she switched it on, surveying which direction might lead to the exit or even the emergency side tunnel. Had that been the way Stefano had extricated himself?

There was a possible opening that she thought she could squeeze through, but she needed both hands free, yet she must carry both torch and the sketch-case. She pushed the latter inside the top part of her boilersuit, then fortunately found a piece of string in the pocket and tried to tie the torch to her helmet to make a miner's light. This was more difficult than she had imagined and finally she slung the torch round her neck, using it only to illumine her route.

Grunting and straining she managed to climb through the opening between the wall and the fallen rocks and scrambled down the other side. Here the passage was easier, for not so much of the tunnel had collapsed and some of the steel arch supports still held.

"Stefano!" she began to call again.

Then she stopped clambering abruptly. She had come the wrong way and was almost outside the tomb chamber.

The thought sent a shudder down her spine. All she had done was land herself in an even more inaccessible place for possible rescuers—if any rescuers ever came.

She was tired and spent. It had been a strenuous day and evening. She rested against a more comfortable piece of rock wall and must have dozed, for when she awoke with a start, her watch indicated that it was nearly four o'clock.

Did anyone know that she was trapped? Surely Stefano must have found someone to help. In a couple of hours the whole staff of workmen would be coming to the site.

Antonia knew what she must do. She must wriggle through the narrow opening again, for no grown man would be able to do so. Every movement was an agony in her exhausted state, and when finally she was through on the return journey, she succeeded in dropping the torch on the wrong side of the stone barrier. She resigned herself to the dark and reassured herself that the precious sketches were still safely with her.

The air seemed to be getting stuffier, but perhaps

that was only her fancy, the fancy of all people who are immured. She tried to fight off sleep so that if she heard voices or any noise she could answer, but she must have slept. All was well, though, for she was in a small boat with Talbot going to the island in Lake Trasimeno. How fresh the breeze, the wide expanse of blue water stretched like silk, the warm sun beating down on her neck and shoulders.

She blinked her eyes open and realised the difference between dream and reality. Now there was nothing but blackness and silence. But another dream took possession of her. There were shouts and bangs and someone calling "Tonia!" and although she kept shouting back, the voices came no nearer. Then there were further crashings and someone again saying, "Tonia darling! Oh, my love, you're safe!"

Still she could not answer, but felt herself lifted and carried, the voices rose to a hubbub, then died in silence, leaving only that whispered, "Tonia my darling," sounding in her ears.

She awoke—and found herself staring at a pale awning. When she raised her head a little she saw a bright patch of blue sky.

"Where—?" she began. "What happened?"

Cleo was kneeling by Antonia's side. "Take it gently," she said. "You're probably still shocked and dazed."

"Yes, the tunnel. It fell down—and I've ruined everything for Talbot."

"Don't worry about him. He can look after his own worries," retorted Cleo.

"One of my worries is right here now," said another voice. Suddenly Cleo's beautiful face was replaced in Antonia's limited vision by Talbot's.

"Oh, Talbot!" she whispered brokenly. "I've spoilt it all for you, after you'd worked so hard. I'm sorry about it." To her utter shame she burst into great tearing sobs and the tears rained down her cheeks.

"Don't cry, my love. It's enough that you're safe."

He gathered her into his arms and held her face against him.

When her tears had subsided, she said, "I only wanted to help you. The sketches—"

"My God! To think you risked your life for those sketches! Why on earth didn't you wait until I could take you through the tunnel?"

"I persuaded Stefano—oh, is he safe?"

Talbot nodded. "He's safe enough. I've given him a piece of my mind to chew on—but I must also be grateful that he wasted no time in sending for help. Now, no more talking. You must rest. We have an ambulance coming out and you must be checked up at the hospital first."

"I'm all right." She smiled at him. "I'm in the tent 'Agincourt' and I'm with you."

He kissed her sweetly and tenderly. "Oh! You didn't take it amiss that time. I might try another."

"Who am I to stop you?" Her eyes danced.

"That's better." This time his kiss was hard and demanding and she found it exquisite to yield.

Cleo poked her head into the tent to say that the ambulance was here.

Now reaction set in for Antonia and she had only the haziest recollection of the drive to hospital, the nurses hovering around, the heads being nodded, a long sleep, and then she was in her room at the Hotel Margharita and the place was filled with flowers.

Talbot came in, his fair hair brushed, his blue eyes alight with that tender look that no girl can mistake.

"Ah, you look cleaner than when I last saw you," he greeted her.

She laughed. "I must have looked a sight!"

"You did. When we hauled you out, you were indeed the worse for wear." He sat by the bedside and took her hand in his own.

She turned her head away for a moment. "I've been a trouble to you almost from the beginning."

"You certainly have," he agreed grimly, holding her

hand more tightly. "I made up my mind years ago that my kind of work didn't fit in with women."

"Yes, you said you refused to be cluttered."

"But you did just that. You cluttered me up in knots, Tonia."

"Not deliberately."

He shook his head in mock sorrow. "However it was done, it was done thoroughly—and for good. I thought that if I succeeded with one good resounding find, one that an eminent museum would be glad to possess, I'd be happy for the rest of my life. But you spoilt all that, Tonia. You made my work come second best, because I couldn't think of any future without you to share it."

"I'm sorry, Talbot," she said, her eyes downcast so that he should not perceive them twinkling.

"Rubbish! You're not sorry at all." He put his finger under her chin and tilted her face upwards. "Don't you want to marry me?"

"Yes, please," she said in a small voice, then flung her arms around his neck. "Oh, Talbot, I was going away because I couldn't bear to stay here and think that you—you didn't want me."

"Idiot! I couldn't get near you. Every time I thought I was breaking down the barrier between us, you shoved it up again. That day at Gubbio—"

"The Feast of the Candles," she murmured.

"It was going fine until Robert came along."

"And Cleo?" she teased.

"Cleo can look after herself. She's tougher than you, Tonia. She took credit for work you'd done on those pots and I blamed you for carelessness. Then she tattled to the press."

He picked up her hand and kissed her finger tips one by one. "Forgive me?"

"So I suppose I won't be going to Naples after all," she said thoughtfully.

"Not without me," he threatened.

"I must tell Philip—and, of course, my mother—"

"I told Philip before he went back to England."

"That you wanted to marry me? What did he say?"

"What d'you think he said? Go ahead. So I have. He was quite a help, your godfather."

There was a long pause between them. Several kisses later she asked, "What about the tunnel? Is it ruined?"

"Not in the least. Actually, you and Stefano may have saved all our lives. We knew that another tunnel had been dug from a different direction, robbers at some time or other, most likely. In places it was above the ceiling of ours and we didn't realise there was a thin crust between. It could have collapsed any time. But we shall soon have it all in good shape again."

"And Stefano? You're not going to sack him, are you?"

Talbot grinned. "In other circumstances, I might, but he's too valuable to me now."

"Don't blame him. Say I tempted him—for friendship's sake, not money."

"You tempted me, too—and I couldn't resist you. So I'll forgive Stefano."

Next day Antonia had recovered sufficiently to be able to go out with Talbot as far as the Perugian "balcony," in the square that overlooked the plain.

"I forgot to tell you," he said, "That your sketches of those fake Etruscan pieces of jewellery and so on have been of immense value. I passed on my information to the museum authorities in Florence and the police have now traced a nice little kiln near Lake Trasimeno, where an artistic gang was turning out pottery and goldsmiths' ware and getting very handsome prices. So at the moment, thanks to you, I'm the museum's white-headed boy."

"And my sketches of the hypogeum newly discovered by that same white-headed boy? No use?"

He held her hand. "When we have time, I'll take you to the director of the museum here. Your sketches are going to be preserved and, in due course, exhibited as the first evidence, apart from photographs, of the interior of the new addition to Perugia's treasures. The

Drurys are going to be quite a respected name in these parts."

Cleo and Robert came to join them. "We hope we don't intrude," said Cleo in her most mincing voice, "but we came to warn you, Talbot, that Tonia is not at her strongest and must be taken care of. See that she doesn't get a chill."

Talbot gave her a mocking bow. "Your orders shall be obeyed. At once."

"Robert and I are going for a walk," Cleo continued. "I've no car until it's repaired, thanks to your excavations—"

"Look at the damage you did to my excavations!"

"That's all you cared about. Robert doesn't want to use his car, so we'll clatter over the cobbles."

"We'll go down to the Etruscan Gate," suggested Robert and Cleo linked her arm in his.

As Talbot and Antonia watched them move away, Antonia said, "The Etruscan Gate works magic for young people. Perhaps Cleo will sense it. I hope so, for Robert's sake."

"The Etruscan Gate was my undoing that first night I met you," he said, putting his arm around her shoulders, as they walked back to the Margharita. "I should have stayed away—"

"But I'm glad you didn't," she whispered.

THE END

To our devoted Harlequin Readers:
Fill in handy coupon below and send off this page.

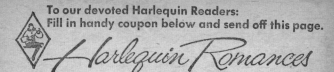

Harlequin Romances

TITLES STILL IN PRINT

- [ ] 51122 WHISTLE AND I'LL COME, Flora Kidd
- [ ] 51123 THE SEA WAIF, Anne Weale
- [ ] 51124 THE NEW ZEALANDER, Joyce Dingwell
- [ ] 51125 DARLING RHADAMANTHUS, Margery Hilton
- [ ] 51126 MAN OF THE ISLANDS, Henrietta Reid
- [ ] 51127 THE BLUE ROSE, Esther Wyndham
- [ ] 51129 MY FRIEND, DOCTOR JOHN, Marjorie Norrell
- [ ] 51130 DALTON'S DAUGHTER, Kate Starr
- [ ] 51132 DARK HORSE, DARK RIDER, Elizabeth Hoy
- [ ] 51134 THE MAN WHO CAME BACK, Pamela Kent
- [ ] 51135 THERE WILL COME A STRANGER, Dorothy Rivers
- [ ] 51137 DOCTOR AT DRUMLOCHAN, Iris Danbury
- [ ] 51138 LOVING IS GIVING, Mary Burchell
- [ ] 51139 THE HOUSE OF MY ENEMY, Norrey Ford
- [ ] 51140 THE MAN IN HOMESPUN, Margaret Malcolm
- [ ] 51141 THE VALLEY OF DESIRE, Catherine Airlie

MAIL THIS COUPON TODAY

Harlequin Books, Dept. Z
Simon & Schuster, Inc., 11 West 39th St.
New York, N.Y. 10018

- [ ] Please send me information about Harlequin Romance Subscribers Club.

Send me titles checked above. I enclose .50 per copy plus .10 per book for postage and handling.

Name ....

Address ....

City................... State .... Zip............